COWGIRL FALLIN' FOR THE MILLER BROTHER

BRIDES OF MILLER RANCH, N.M. BOOK 4

NATALIE DEAN

DEDICATION

I'd like to dedicate this book to YOU! The readers of my books. Without your interest in reading these heartwarming stories of love, I wouldn't have made it this far. So thank you so much for taking the time to read any and hopefully all of my books.

And I can't leave out my wonderful mother, son, sister, and Auntie. I love you all, and thank you for helping me make this happen.

Most of all, I thank God for blessing me on this endeavor.

AND... I've got a special team of advance readers who are always so helpful in pointing out any last minute corrections that need to be made. I'm so thankful to those of you who are so helpful!

BRIDES OF MILLER RANCH, N.M.

Miller Family Saga Series 3

Cowgirl Fallin' for the Single Dad

Cowgirl Fallin' for the Ranch Hand

Cowgirl Fallin' for the Neighbor

Cowgirl Fallin' for the Miller Brother

Cowgirl Fallin' for Her Best Friend's Brother

Cowboy Fallin' in Love Again

Brides of Miller Ranch Complete Collection

Miller Family Wrap-up Story

(An update on all your favorite characters!)

Copper Creek Romances

BAKER BROTHERS OF COPPER CREEK

Copper Creek Romances Series 1

Cowboys & Protective Ways

Cowboys & Crushes

Cowboys & Christmas Kisses

Cowboys & Broken Hearts

Cowboys & Second Chances

Cowboys & Wedding Woes

Cowboys' Mom Finds Love

Baker Brothers of Copper Creek Complete Collection

CALLAHANS OF COPPER CREEK

Copper Creek Romances Series 2

Making a Cowgirl

Marrying a Cowgirl

Christmas with a Cowgirl

Trusting a Cowgirl

Dating a Cowgirl

Catching a Cowgirl

Loving a Cowgirl

Marrying a Cowboy

Callahans of Copper Creek Complete Collection

KEAGANS OF COPPER CREEK

Copper Creek Romances Series 3

Some Cowboys are Off-Limits

Some Cowgirls Love Single Dads

Some Cowboys are Infuriating

Some Cowboys Don't Like City Girls

Some Cowboys Heal Broken Hearts

Some Cowgirls are Worth Protecting

Some Cowboys are Just Friends (Coming August 2024)

Though I try to keep this list updated in each book, you may also visit
my website nataliedeanauthor.com for the most up to date information
on my book list.

CONTENTS

1

————

Charlie

"Hey, Charlie! Your phone is going off!"

Charlie looked up from the tire he'd just been patching to see Clara standing on the porch, his phone in her flour-covered hand.

"Oh, sorry. Didn't even realize I'd left it behind!" Putting the tire aside, he jogged over to his sister and took the blue, thick case from her. "I guess I'm lucky this didn't end up in the oven."

"Yeah, I'm pretty sure that would void the warranty," Clara said with a chuckle before heading in.

A quick check of his screen told him it was Raph, his rodeo friend who was in town every summer and stayed in contact via texting the rest of the year. Grin already on his face, Charlie answered the call.

"Hey there! Long time, no talk."

"I'm sorry about that, Charlie. Things have been kinda crazy this year."

"Have they?"

He didn't know why he phrased his question like that. Although Charlie wasn't familiar with all of the comings and goings of the rodeo he occasionally worked for, he had heard about plenty of drama that had happened during the fall and winter circuits.

"I know we talked about it kinda jokingly, or kinda like a 'what if' scenario, but were you serious about being willing to help the rodeo out? We just had one of our subs fall through, and you know how hard it is to get a reliable person on short notice."

"I'd have to think on it a minute. It sounds like it'd be fun, but it gets busy during the summer on the ranch."

"I know, I know. I just figured with you telling me about that guy your sister hired that maybe you could justify it. Even coming on part-time would be a huge help. You're one of the best clowns around these parts and the animals like you a whole bunch."

Perhaps in any other situation that would be an insult, but considering that Charlie volunteered as an actual rodeo clown, it was quite the compliment. He loved the adrenaline of ducking out of the way just in time. And helping distract an animal so it didn't hurt a rider made him feel important. Like he was protecting a comrade. Sure, that was probably overly dramatic, but his sisters couldn't hog all of the grand fantasies.

"Alright, I definitely think I could do that."

"Really, man? You'd be on board?"

"I need some more details, scheduling and all that, but yeah. I can't talk much about this right now though, we're about to have this big family thing this afternoon."

"Oh, sorry. I didn't mean to interrupt."

But Charlie just chuckled gently. "Don't worry about it. I know you don't ever call me unless it's important, and we're still getting ready anyway. It's kinda crazy here though. I haven't had to deal with a preteen's birthday in a long time."

Raph chuckled too. "She's your oldest sister's kid, right?"

A warm feeling filled Charlie's heart. "Not her kid yet, although she might as well be. Savannah is her boyfriend's kid from his first marriage."

"Right, right, I think I remember that now. But man, I think it's cool how your sister just took over. A lot of people wouldn't embrace a preteen with open arms. You know how complicated kids are."

"Thankfully, I don't. Not really."

"Hah, right. Still holding on to that no dating streak?"

"I've got other things on my plate."

"Like birthday parties for little girls?"

"Exactly."

We shared a laugh and then my friend let out a long sigh of relief. "Well, I'll let you get back to it, but you're a life saver man. For real."

"I do my best. Be safe, bozo."

"You too, Bible-boy."

He hung up and Charlie headed back inside. He wouldn't normally let anyone talk to him like that, but he and Raph went so far back that their teasing nicknames were layered with more love than mockery. And it wasn't like he was overflowing with long-term friends after all.

It wasn't that it was hard for him to make friends, not at all. Clara had remarked at least a dozen times in the past year how he could just walk up to someone and start a conversation.

Charity reminded him regularly that although his charms worked plenty outside of the house, they didn't fool her.

It was just that, on the whole, Charlie didn't want more friends. He didn't really want much that wasn't found right on the ranch. And sure, maybe his bubble was small, but it was safe. He felt protected in it and able to work on what he chose, do what he chose, without watching his back.

Granted, a whole lot of people had been added to his bubble lately, something he was reminded of when he spotted Clara putting cupcakes in the oven. Several finished cakes sat cooling on the island behind her.

"Whoa, do you need help with anything here?"

His closest sister whirled, her apricot lips parting in that movie star smile she had. Clara had always been a poised, vintage beauty, but ever since she'd started dating that Nathan fellow, her confidence had blossomed. *Really* blossomed.

Charlie was still wary of Nathan. He was a quiet guy, but there was this undercurrent of anger in him that the Miller brother picked up on every now and then. He was aware that the guy had been through a lot—being struck by lightning and all that—but still... it was difficult to let down his walls and trust him with his sister.

He was trying though.

"Oh, thank goodness! Yes, I absolutely could. Do you mind whipping up some icing for me? You remember how I taught you, right?"

"It's pretty simple."

Charlie was aware that some dudes would be upset or resistant to being taught about confection, but he always liked working with his sisters. Especially when that work resulted in delicious food.

"You look nice, by the way."

"Do I?" she asked, a huge smile on her face and a sparkle in her eyes. "I haven't thrown a kid's party in years. It's been so fun planning and decorating."

I looked around at all the streamers, decorations, and food Clara had all over the house. Of course, she wasn't the only one who had done the work, but she was definitely the mastermind.

"I can see that."

We settled into a companionable sort of quiet until Cass tromped in, her cane hitting the floor fairly hard. I knew that as a sound of exhaustion, and I casually got a chair for her. The stools at the kitchen island were still pretty uncomfortable, even after so much time in PT and progress.

Cass huffed gratefully and practically toppled into the chair. "I never knew pruning tomatoes could be so exhausting."

A laugh sounded from where Clara was looking into the oven. "Do you have tar fingers yet?"

Cass looked down at her hands and let out her own exhausted but amused sound. "Would you look at that. I didn't even notice."

"I'll get you some aloe wipes," Charlie said, retreating to their downstairs bathroom then returning to toss her the pack.

Cass caught it, sending him an appreciative smile.

"Did I mention I love these things? They really help with how irritated my palms get sometimes with my walker and cane."

"Aloe is amazing, isn't it?" Clara hummed a tune, turning the oven down. "Did you know Nathan's been growing a few? They're doing wonderfully."

"Not to abruptly change the subject," Cass said with a nod. "But is that nice librarian lady coming to this party?"

"Of course. Savannah insisted on it."

"Are you sure it's Savannah who insisted?" Cass continued nonchalantly, but Charlie knew her well enough to catch the mischievous glint in her eyes.

"You still trying to hook Papa up with that nice lady?" he asked, turning off his mixer and giving his sister a look.

"What? I can't be the only one who notices the chemistry. She's the first lady that he's gone on a date with in forever."

"Didn't he insist he was just helping her for some fundraiser?"

Now it was Cass's turn to level him with a certified Miller *look*. "And you buy that? Charity doesn't."

"That's because she's the number one fan of the subplot romance you've got going on in your head."

"I'm just *saying*, I'm glad the librarian is coming. She's a nice lady and I like her."

Clara let out another hum. "Of course, you do. That's why you know her name."

"Just because I have a terrible memory doesn't mean that she's not a perfect match for Papa."

Charlie shook his head. He actually agreed with Cass, for the most part, but he liked teasing her. His sisters were sometimes so serious that he couldn't help but try to get them to lighten up.

"All this talk of Papa and he isn't even here to defend himself," he remarked with an impish grin.

"Don't worry. I have no problem dropping hints right in front of him."

"Given Papa, you might need to rent a billboard."

"You might actually have a point there."

They all shared a few examples before returning to their various tasks. But there was a comforting sort of warmth that bubbled up from within Charlie, the one that always came whenever he was able to do things with his siblings.

The world was a scary, dark place with a lot of people who wanted to hurt people just for the fun of it. The ranch, his family, was a safe place where he could just be.

And he wouldn't give it up for the world.

2

———————

Charlie

"Alright, so I know you've helped us plenty, but let me give you the tour of how we've set stuff up this year."

Charlie nodded, taking note whenever the season's boss pointed out something that had changed from the previous year. Although Charlie was plenty familiar with the rodeo, he realized that just volunteering was a much lighter schedule than actually working the circuit. He wasn't mad about it, however. If anything, he was excited for a challenge.

He preferred to stay on the ranch if he could, but the rodeo circuit was familiar enough to also feel like a mostly safe place. Sure, there were rude people sitting in the stands at the rodeo every once in a while, but on the whole it was a great place, and he loved the animals.

"Okay, so we're gonna want you on bull riding, barrels and

mutton busting. You've always been so good with the kid guests. We figured that would be a good spot for you."

"That's not the first time I've heard that," Charlie said with a grin. Sure, he didn't have any children of his own, but he liked them plenty. Back when he was younger, he always envisioned having a big family like the extended Miller families, but then... well, that had certainly been sidelined, hadn't it?

"What about clownin' or playing in the audience?" Charlie wasn't picky, but he liked that part too. Funny, for preferring ranch life, he enjoyed performing for the people attending almost as much as he liked distracting for the riders."

"We'll have you on that sometimes, but mostly you're gonna be in the rings."

"Alright, I can do that."

"Great. We really appreciate this, Charlie. You're saving our bacon more than you know. Training another complete newbie over the two we've already got would be way more than we could handle."

"Ah, well, ... I was around."

"Hardly. Your ranch is a fair drive away from here, right?"

"Barely an hour," he answered with a shrug. "Besides, it's not like my sisters won't visit me weekly."

The boss, Jeremiah, let out a snort. "That's right. The only boy out of five. I don't know how you survived having four sisters."

Charlie liked Jeremiah. He really did. But if there was one thing that really irritated him it was when people acted like his sisters were some sort of hardship. Like Charlie was somehow disadvantaged just because he lived with more women than men, like his cousins. It was plain wrong and he didn't care for it. His sisters and Papa had been his lifeline after Mama had passed, and without them, Charlie was sure he'd have long since fallen apart. He could trust them. Tell them everything.

Well... almost everything.

"What do you mean?" Charlie said, his voice level. He'd found the best way to deal with such comments was to pretend that he didn't understand. Usually, when people had to explain their thoughtless jokes, they realized that they weren't very funny after all.

"Oh, you know what I mean."

"Not really, brother. Can you explain?"

Jeremiah gave him an odd expression, but Charlie kept his face pleasant. He wasn't mad at his boss, but he wanted the man to come to his own conclusion rather than spoon-feeding it to him. "I mean, it had to have been hard, sharing all that space with women."

"Not really. Do you find it hard to spend time with women?"

"What? No! It's just there must have never been a bathroom open, right?"

"Nah. We have two large bathrooms and all our personal bedrooms have at least a half bath."

"Oh um, right. Time to go on lunch. Let me show you where the mess is. We moved it to the opposite side this year."

Charlie nodded, letting it go and hoping Jeremiah would ruminate on why he said that. Maybe he wouldn't, but he'd definitely learned not to say anything bad about the Miller sisters in front of Charlie.

"Hey! Bible-boy!"

Charlie looked over to see Raph sitting at one of the picnic tables, waving enthusiastically. His boss took that opportunity to quickly escape, and Charlie might have laughed if he thought it wasn't the best time for it.

"Hey there, bozo," Charlie shot back. "I see you already found the most important place here."

"You betcha. Life ain't worth living on an empty stomach." Raph clapped his back and led Charlie over to the table.

The mess hall was less a hall and more of a food truck circle, and less of a food truck circle and more like a random smattering of boxy vehicles that meals were cooked in. There were four tall poles in one corner that a tarp could be stretched over in case it rained, but mostly it was a flattened, outdoor area with about five picnic tables and a few of those fold-out ones with cheap chairs. Sure, it wasn't exactly glamourous, but there was fresh TexMex, carnie food and other good fixings.

"Man, you came here just in time. The beauties just rolled up!"

"The beauties?" Charlie echoed, distracted by what smelled like some really good alfredo. Had they added a new truck to the rodeo repertoire?

"Check it out! Is it just me, or are they especially fine this year?"

Charlie looked over to where Raph was jerking his head, and he saw a group of women rodeo workers and riders all sitting down at one of the longer picnic tables. They were pretty, sure, especially since they all seemed to be happily talking with each other. Charlie wasn't particularly close with any of them, but he liked to see people genuinely enjoying themselves.

But then his eyes landed on the woman at their center, who was still standing up and gesticulating emphatically. The people around her were all laughing, and it was clear that she was the star of the table, but that didn't stop Charlie from grimacing and turning back to Raph.

"So, what about that food?"

He wasn't surprised when his friend laughed. "You and Daisy still hate each other, huh?"

"I don't hate her," Charlie replied with a sigh. "I just find her off-putting."

"Man, even when you don't like someone, you're still polite. You're way nicer than me."

"Not a hard bar to get over, my friend."

"And yet you have no problem cutting me down!"

"Maybe 'cause you deserve it."

"I mean, probably. Let's get you your food. You've always been weird about girls anyway."

No.

Not always.

3

Daisy

*B*riiiiinnng!

BRIIIIIIIIIINNNNNGGG!

Daisy groaned, trying to cling to sleep, but the multiple alarms going off on her phone was violently ripping it away.

"Alright, alright, I *get* it."

With a few more groans, Daisy reached out, hand flopping over to try to reach her phone and turn the annoying sound off.

But she couldn't find it, so with a few more choice words, she sat up and looked blearily at her surroundings. She was in her trailer, and her head was throbbing something fierce.

Ugh. She'd drank the night before. It looked like her seven-month sober streak was over. Back to day one again.

"Why do you always do this to yourself?" Daisy grumbled.

It wasn't her fault that the first night back at the rodeo was so fun. She was able to see friends that she hadn't seen in ages and stuff her face with good, cheap food and tons of free beer. But it *was* her fault that she had actually chosen to imbibe. She knew what she was like, and alcohol wasn't for her, and yet...

Drat.

It was just that after working a boring retail job during the winter, she was more than ready to cut loose and perform for the crowd.

But that would have to wait until after she got her hangover under control.

BRIIIIIIIIIIIIIIIIIIIIIIIIIIIIIIIIIIING!!!

Ugh, why had she chosen to set her alarm to escalate with every new set of rings?

Oh right, because even after years of working the circuit, she was still a night owl, so she needed a full-scale assault on her eardrums to wake up.

After more grumbling, she forced herself out of bed and grabbed her shower kit, stumbling out of her tiny sleeper trailer as she rubbed her eyes. Not every rodeo she'd worked at had a communal shower built for the workers. But thankfully, this one did. It was one of the reasons she stuck with it from early spring all the way to the close of winter. She didn't have any sort of plumbing in her tiny little sleeper, and she lived several hours away, so it would have been impossible to run to the gym she had a membership at to shower. Sure, the communal showers were ramshackle and in a literal shack, but they got her clean.

Her headache eased as she went through her morning routine. The cool water definitely helped, especially at her temples where so much of the pounding was gathered. Once more, she swore to herself that she wasn't ever going to get drunk again, even if she knew she was going to break that promise in a day or two.

But promises or not, she brushed her teeth with her fingers, using a generous amount of toothpaste to make up for her lack of a toothbrush. She was going to buy a real one, she really was, but that had to wait until her next paycheck when she rode into town on a Monday.

No one wanted to come to a rodeo on a Monday, so that was when most of the workers got their personal stuff done. It was also the day after most of their direct deposits hit, so it was the best time to shop for necessities.

Teeth squeaky clean, Daisy stretched and headed back to her mini-trailer. Her clothes hamper grabbed her attention when she entered. She'd been so tired that she hadn't really had a chance to put her clothes away after hitting up the laundromat. It was about time for her to go again, given the growing pile of dirty clothes in the trash bag on the passenger's seat of her truck.

Oh well. Another thing that needed to wait until she was paid.

Sighing, Daisy tucked all that away and headed to get breakfast with the other late risers. Being that a lot of the rodeo crew were farmers, it wasn't uncommon for them to be up at six AM. That was a big 'no thank you' from Daisy. Eight in the morning was about as early as her internal clock went, and that was that.

At least there was plenty of good food available, and for super cheap. Daisy could get a solid stomach full for just two dollars, and it would keep her satiated until she could finally eat in the afternoon again.

"Hey there, girlie girl. You look *rough*."

Daisy didn't have to look to know it was her coworker and

friend, Melinda. "Hey, you know the rules, no mocking me before my caffeine."

"Well, it's a good thing I've got two cups of coffee in my hand, isn't it?"

That made Daisy whirl, and sure enough, her friend was already holding out a blessed, delicious cup of joe.

"You are a scholar and a gentleman," Daisy said, taking the cup and gulping it down. "Ahhh, that hits the spot!"

"Glad you like it. Made it on my hot plate myself."

"No one makes trailer joe like you, my friend."

"And don't you forget it." Melinda linked arms with her and walked them toward their usual breakfast spot, a rusted old food truck run by Gertie McMillion. She was a plump, older lady who made the best hangover cures and pancakes. "You hit that bottle pretty hard last night, darling. Color me nosey, but aren't you supposed to be permanently broken up with the devil's drink?"

Daisy sighed. She'd been doing good for so long, but it was just so hard to escape the stress sometimes, especially if everyone around her was partaking. "It's more of an off-again, on-again relationship."

"My cousin was in one of those. Sounds pretty awful."

Daisy squinted, the sunlight around them making her head pound. "It's not great."

"Do you need a ride-along buddy, or do you need some space? Cause, I'm about as stubborn as a mule and—"

Daisy gave her friend a half-hearted smile as she cut her off. It was true, Melinda would probably be great at helping her stay sober again for another streak, but it was far too embarrassing to be a babysitter. Daisy was a big girl. She could take care of herself.

Sometimes...

"Nah, I'm good, friend. Thank you."

"Alright then. I trust you." And that was that. If there was one thing that Daisy would never get over, it was how Melinda just went with the flow and didn't think she automatically knew better than everyone around her.

"By the by, last comment, but it wouldn't hurt to spruce yourself up a little. Especially with that handsome millionaire coming around again. He's single, you know." She waggled her eyebrows, letting Daisy know she was mostly poking fun.

"Millionaire?"

Daisy looked to where her friend was subtly pointing, only to see a familiar figure sitting at a table with a couple of his friends. They were talking animatedly, still full of all the energy that came from the start of the season, with one at the center clearly leading the conversation.

"Oh. *Him.*" Daisy rolled her eyes, knowing her nose was scrunching with distaste, but it wasn't like she could help it.

"Right, I forgot. Why is it that you two hate each other so much?"

"I don't *hate* him," Daisy said with a sigh. She made it a point to try to get along with everyone she worked with, but some of the part-timers and volunteers were annoying. Either because they didn't know anything or they didn't take her seriously, and she just didn't have time for that.

"Well, what is it?"

"I don't get why some hoity-toity rich, arrogant guy does this. It's like he's slummin' it with us for fun. I dunno... seems suspect."

But of course, Melinda just rolled her eyes. "Gosh, you're so cynical."

"Maybe I am, but am I ever wrong?"

Melinda sounded like she wanted to argue, but then Gert was yelling for the next person and Daisy was finally able to get her breakfast without any talk of spoiled playboys.

She doubted Mr. Charlie Miller ever had to meticulously count down his last seven dollars to make sure he could eat at least once a day.

4

———

Charlie

"I'm going to take the right exit. You take the left. Remember which bull it is?"

Charlie nodded. "Big Red. He tends to favor turning left and has a slow turn."

"You got it." Rick sent him a big grin even though two of his teeth were missing. "First show of the season is always exciting, isn't it?"

"It is," Charlie confirmed, straightening his clown outfit. "Ready for some adrenaline?"

"I sure am." There was a pause and Charlie thought that was that, but then Rick was clearing his throat. "Say, your sisters gonna visit this weekend?"

"Usually at least one of them shows up."

"That's awesome." Another pause and this time Charlie had a feeling that wasn't the end of it. "Is uh... is Clara gonna be one of them?"

Ah, so *that's* what it was about.

"I'm sorry, mate, but Clara's spoken for."

It was borderline humorous to see the myriad of emotions flick across Rick's face. Surprise, sadness, and then maybe a little chagrin. "I should have guessed. A lady like that is one of a kind." He heaved a sigh before perking up ever so slightly. "And she's happy?"

It was sweet, in a way. Rick was a good guy, as far as Charlie knew. He'd worked with the man for the past two years and he was always polite. Always respectful.

"She's very happy."

"Wish her the best, I do."

Charlie waited a moment, wondering if he was going to ask about any of the other Miller girls, but the man seemed like he was already getting into concentration mode. Maybe it was strange, but that made Charlie smile.

In his twenty-odd years of life, Charlie had run the gamut with men's reactions to his sisters, and every now and then someone would treat them like they were interchangeable. Those guys always turned him off. Someone who fell in love with Charity couldn't fall in love with Clara, and the perfect man for Cass wasn't going to work with Cici at all.

Not to mention Cici was the baby of the family, and Charlie would throw fists if anyone made her uncomfortable.

But thankfully, Rick wasn't anything like that, and that affirmed to Charlie that he was with good people. And it was with that feeling of comfort that he went over to his spot, ready for the bull run.

And it was perfect.

The rider lasted a good while, really riling the crowd up. The programmers hadn't put their best rider first, but they had put one of the better ones. Charlie appreciated that they had an excellent sense of drama. The rodeo had perfected the rhythm of a hired rider, then a local rider who'd paid an entrance fee, then a hired rider again. The show certainly was a lot more fun that way.

But the cowboy couldn't last forever, and eventually he fell off. That was Charlie's cue, and he rushed in with Rick, distracting the bull. He dipped, he dodged, and he scrambled up the sides whenever Big Red got too close. He and Rick were able to keep the bull pretty caught up between the two of them until the rider was able to get clear, and then they led the creature back into his pen.

The crowd was roaring, laughing, and clapping just like they were supposed to, and it played out well. Big Red's owners were already waiting to feed and calm down their guy, but judging by the grins on their faces, they could hear the rancor too.

The rest of the day went pretty fast. After the show, Charlie made a round thanking the bulls and patting their backs, then it was off to get food. He had to wash his makeup off first—being a clown came with slathering his face with grease paint, after all—so he headed for the showers. Charlie was so distracted texting his sisters about where to meet that he didn't notice the line at the showers until he almost ran into it.

"Whoa, sorry there."

The figure turned, and of course it was *her*.

None other than Daisy, aka Scarlet. She was wearing one of her bedazzled riding outfits but half of it was caked in mud, with a good amount of it caked into her thick, wild hair. She was one of the few women riders Charlie knew who rode with her hair loose, and he guessed it was because it leant to her 'fiery' persona.

Because, as unfortunate as it was, Scarlet was a real crowd favorite. And even more unfortunately, Charlie got exactly why. She was gregarious and knew how to perform with the best of them. She never failed to get a crowd going and had a real way with animals.

But Charlie still didn't like her.

"Oh, it's you," she said flatly. "Have fun clowning around?"

Her tone was perfectly level, but Charlie didn't miss the hostility. "Sure did. Did you have fun playing in the dirt?"

"'Fraid not, this is from hard work. But it's okay that you don't recognize that."

"Funny, it feels like I get paid to play every day compared to a hard day working on the ranch."

She snorted at that, rolling her eyes as she faced forward. "Uh-huh, I'm sure your life is a real trial."

Ugh.

Somehow, she still kept her tone banal and pleasant, plain, simple and devoid of any emotion. And yet... she still managed to convey an absolutely scathing meaning, nonetheless.

He didn't know why he let her get under his skin. He'd heard a lot worse from a lot meaner people. But it was something about her complete dismissal that rubbed him the wrong way. That, and the fact that she swore as often as she didn't, and half the time when he saw her after the sun went down, she was drunk. He'd long since learned that he didn't want to be around most people who were drunk, and even Daisy's charisma and good looks didn't overcome that personal boundary for him.

So, the two of them stood there, in utter silence, until finally

Charlie's sisters texted him back. Charity and Clara had both managed to make it and wanted to eat at a BBQ place about twenty minutes away. Thankfully, with eight stalls, the line went quickly, and Charlie was able to take a stall on the farthest side from where he saw Daisy head. He knew some people would be scandalized with women and men showering in the same place, but each stall was completely separate, and everyone was respectful.

...after hours, maybe less so, but Charlie always went straight to his trailer after that.

His trailer was a new addition to his life that he was particularly jazzed about. After seeing Mick's trailer at the ranch and how convenient it was, he'd decided to buy his own RV. He hadn't had any set plans for it at first, but once Raph had extended the invitation to work full-time, it was hard not to feel like he'd definitely been led by some divine providence.

But the water hadn't been hooked up to his RV yet, so he was still stuck using the communal showers for another couple of days. Not that he minded. The cool water was nice, and he was able to get most of his grease paint off without too much hassle, then hurry to his siblings.

"Hey there, rodeo champ," Charity said, waving.

"You were so cool!" Savannah said from beside her, jumping up and down. Somehow the young girl had managed to grow another two inches, and Charlie was pretty sure she was going to outpace Clara. "You didn't look scared of that bull at all."

"Because I wasn't," Charlie said, opening his arms for the young girl to hug him. And, like usual, she threw herself at him. Charlie caught her, spinning her around before setting her on her feet.

At first, although he'd liked the girl, he wasn't quite comfortable with how physical she was. Savannah was a sweet child, and she loved to hold hands, high five, hug and otherwise be physically affectionate. And that wasn't a bad thing, not at all, but it had been a *lot* for him at first. Thankfully, with over two years in each other's circles, Charlie had had plenty of time to warm up to her and now he accepted her as blood.

"How weren't you scared?"

"Because I respect the bull, and I know it's language."

"It's language?"

"All animals have a way of talking. You just have to learn it."

There was a quiet laugh from Clara. "Are you stealing my lines now?"

"Well, you say them often enough."

Clara ruffled his hair, something he only tolerated because he loved her, and then they were off. Savannah was a bundle of energy of course, and Charlie was pleased when he found out that it was her first rodeo. At first, he didn't know how that was possible. Then he remembered that she'd moved from Cali, and with her father being a doctor establishing his practice, they hadn't exactly had a lot of time to explore the attractions and events in the area.

Except for the fall festival. Savannah *loved* the fall festival. Which was impressive considering that her first event had ended in her witnessing a brawl between several of the Miller siblings and some drunk town losers.

But even with Savannah's constant streams of exclamations and questions, Charlie had a great dinner with his sisters. Apparently, Papa, Mick and Cass were going to try to swing out the next weekend, and the following, Cici. He couldn't believe that she was about to return for summer break. The years were going by so fast, and she was going to be the first Miller of their part of the extended family to actually complete their degree. Charlie had tried, but...

Well, he knew exactly how that had turned out.

5

____

Daisy

aisy popped a couple more ibuprofen and flopped back, settling her heating pad on her sore muscles. Opening weekend took a toll on her body as it got used to the rigor of rodeo work.

"Ugh, where did I put my chocolate?"

Fumbling around at the base of her mattress, she found her cheap, dollar store chocolate on the floor. It was the fake stuff, but it was way better than nothing, that was for sure. Daisy wasn't the biggest on sweets, but when it came to opening weekend, she really needed something to help her through.

And some red meat. Her mouth watered at the thought of a nice, juicy steak, but that wasn't going to happen anytime soon. Daisy couldn't remember the last time she'd been able to afford something like that.

But eventually. Or at least that was what she kept telling herself. If she worked hard and applied herself and could just go three months without some sort of hiccup, she would be fine.

She just wished her body didn't hurt so badly.

Daisy tried to lay there with her heating pad as long as she could, but eventually her hunger pangs got the better of her.

Groaning—she seemed to be doing that all the time lately— she sat up and went to the mini-fridge tucked against the wall. Her trailer was tiny, barely big enough for the twin mattress she had on the floor, plus her laundry basket, her mini-fridge, her microwave and her hot plate, but it was enough. It kept her warm, it kept her safe, and it saved her a whole lot of money on rent.

Sure, she still had to pay car insurance and the like, but what was the point in keeping an apartment she only spent two or three months out of the year in? She'd have more room, yeah, but even less money, and Daisy didn't want to go back to being *that* broke.

She wasn't rich, but she had been worse, and she gratefully grabbed a frozen meal out of the freezer portion of her fridge and popped it into the microwave. She had spent the two dollars she'd planned for her meal on getting ibuprofen from the gas station down the road, so she'd have to stick to her emergency provisions for that night. And the next if she wanted to have enough until her first payment cleared at the bank. She knew that Gert and a few others would spot her—none of them would ever let a worker go hungry—but her situation wasn't desperate enough for her to ask that.

...yet.

The microwave dinged and Daisy opened the door, cutting the plastic and stirring the ingredients as she was supposed to.

The thing didn't look very appetizing, but her favorite pasta and broccoli ones had been out the last time she went to the store, so she'd had to resort to alternate meals. Besides, they all kind of tasted the same after a while, and Daisy knew a full belly was more important than the food actually being delicious.

Once it was done, she let it sit for the three minutes the directions always asked for.

Goodness, she wanted a beer something fierce, but she was supposed to be back on her sober schtick. As hard as it was, she really did like herself better when she and alcohol were far, far away from each other. Between spending too much on booze, drinking herself into embarrassing situations, and being punished with stomach problems and severe hangovers, her life was obviously better without any sort of libations.

...but she really, *really* wanted a drink.

But then another vicious muscle cramp hit her. *Owwww.* Was this her punishment for getting a hangover the previous day? It kinda seemed like it.

Daisy stood there, trying to slowly breathe in and out, but a knock on the door interrupted her before she could spiral. Straightening up, she opened the door of her trailer and was surprised to see Melinda, Esperanza, and Billy all standing just outside her mini-home.

"Oh hey, what's up? Did I forget we were supposed to meet up?" she asked, her eyes going to the bags hanging from several of their arms.

"Hey there, babe! I noticed you rushed off right after that shift and that wasn't like you. You doing okay?"

Daisy couldn't help but give her friend a warm smile. It had been months since they'd last interacted, and yet they clicked into place like no time had passed at all. "I'm alright. It's just sore muscles from opening weekend."

"Oh *geez*. I hear you. You really go all out in the ring. You sure you're alright?"

"Do you need something stronger?" Esperanza said, concern in her voice. "I got something stronger from the doctor. You should look into it, Daisy."

"I'll think on it," Daisy said. It wasn't that she had anything against seeking medical help; it was just she already had so much hospital debt that she didn't want to add a single dime to it. Plus, that was the last thing she needed—something else to get addicted to. "But thank y'all for checking up on me. I've got food, caffeine, chocolate and my heating pad, so I'll be alright."

"Pfffft, nah girl, we got the fixings for a good night here. Junk food, soda, some non-alcoholic beer and sparkling grape juice, and Bill sprung for some fresh ground burger. You grab your blankie and we'll fix everything up at Esperanza's camp."

"Wow, really? You didn't have to do that, guys."

But Melinda just grinned. "The rodeo is family. That's what we're here for."

Daisy hugged her friend, almost dropping her heating pad, before rushing to do what Melinda had said. A lot of terrible things happened in Daisy's life but finding her family at the rodeo wasn't one of them.

In fact, she was pretty sure she wouldn't be alive without them.

6

Charlie

Charlie was having a *great* time.

It turned out that working full-time at the rodeo was actually pretty fulfilling. Sure, Charlie missed the ranch, especially after a few weeks passed, but he also felt like he was practically at home.

Except home didn't have exciting performances complete with hundreds of people cheering for him.

His siblings attended every weekend, and although Cici had been delayed in returning home, she was going to be flying in the next weekend. Papa had come twice and even paid for a catered meal for the entire crew. That had certainly been a popular move with everyone.

Well, everyone but Daisy.

It wasn't that she made a big deal of it, or anything. And she was certainly there helping herself to the food, but while she thanked Papa, she hadn't even so much as looked at Charlie. It was a deliberate snub, obviously, but it wasn't really rude enough to complain about. And when he did bother to gripe to one of his sisters, he was promptly told that just because someone wasn't charmed by him, that didn't mean that they were insulting him.

Charlie begged to differ. He wasn't full of himself by any means. But he was good guy. Why did she dislike him so much?

But Daisy aside, it was one of the best summers he'd had since Cass's injury, and it was a long time coming. Charlie hadn't quite realized it, but with his sister's relationship drama, then Cass's accident, there'd been a sort of heavy cloak over the family. A heavy, *depressing* cloak. And while Charity, Cass, and Clara had found their ways out from under it, Charlie had been content to linger there. Maybe it was because of the familiarity. Maybe it was because he had just gotten used to it. But spending so much time away from the ranch doing something he loved reminded him what it was like to be relatively normal.

"Hey, Bible-boy, you coming?"

"Yeah, give me a minute, bozo. I just want to brush my hair."

Raph huffed from where he was sitting in the cushioned egg-chair in Charlie's extended RV. "Please, who are you primping for? It's not like you pay attention to any of the fine ladies here."

"It's about being presentable," Charlie shot back. "Women don't just do their makeup for men, and I don't brush my hair for anyone else but me."

Raph had grown his hair out long enough to keep it braided in a traditional indigenous style. But Charlie's hair was thick and somewhere between curly and wiry, so it required at least a little maintenance every once in a while.

"Women don't—is that one of those weird things that comes from having all sisters?"

"If you mean it's one of the things I learned from actually listening to women, then yes."

"What's the use of being so smooth with the ladies if you never use your moves?"

"Let's just go to the dinner, shall we?"

When he was part-time, Charlie would always go home before the after-weekend party would happen, having about zero interest in sticking around any sort of raucous shindig that involved drinking and loud people. But after working full-time with the other rodeo folks, he'd taken to liking those rowdy get-togethers. Sure, there were the occasional arguments or drama, but on the whole, it was a good time.

"Maybe Fernando made those margaritas again. Those things were *good*."

"Mm-hmm."

Thankfully, Charlie managed to herd Raph out of the door and head to the events. Music was already playing and multiple people were either in their pajamas or lounge wear as they ate, danced, or played various games. It probably looked strange to any outsider, but to Charlie it made sense. They all worked hard every day, dealing with the audience, the contests, the cleaning and the animals. When a week wore down and it was finally Sunday night, that was the time to let loose and celebrate the success of five days of work.

"Ayyy, Charlaaaay! I noticed your sister Clara came by on Saturday," Rick said, approaching him and offering him a beer. Charlie shook his head and Rick didn't remark on it, which was a relief. "She had a tall, handsome fellow with her. That her guy?"

"No, that was Mick with her, Cass's man."

"Your sister Cass is dating too? I'm glad to hear that. I know that accident knocked her for a real loop."

"It did," Charlie said with a nod. "But why did you want to know?"

"I'm as red-blooded as the next guy, but gosh, there was something about that man. Made me feel self-conscious, which is silly, I know, but I'm four beers in so now it seems real important."

Charlie felt a wave of admiration for the man. He was handling rejection fairly well, and that was more rare than he knew. And Mick was a stunningly handsome sort of man, the kind you might see on a magazine cover.

"You'll know Clara's man if you see him."

"If? He ain't gonna attend the rodeo with his lady? It ain't right to let her always go alone."

"Well, he's recovering from being in the hospital so—"

"Geez, now I feel like a heel."

"It's okay. I know you just want to make sure she's treated right. But trust me, if my sister was being mistreated, I'd be on his hind in an instant."

"You're a good brother." Rick slung an arm around his shoulder. "That's why I like you. I mean, I like yer whole family. Sometimes I think I just need to find a nice farm girl and uh... *settle*. Right, settle down, you know? Make a family."

"That's an admirable dream, Rick."

"It is, isn't it? But why ain't you found a lady yet? You're handsome, you've got all your teeth, and you're rich as sin."

Oh boy. Carefully, Charlie extracted himself from his friend's arm. "Hey, I gotta go hit the facilities. Keep my boy Raph company, alright?"

"More like give your boy Raph some beer."

Charlie chuckled as he trotted off to the bathroom. While he was enjoying the party, he still needed to take breaks every once and a while. Usually because sometimes it was easier to run away than try to explain his various quirks.

He lingered by the portable potties, far enough away that the scent of them didn't get to him, before heading back. But on his way, he heard something just out of place enough for him to slow to a stop.

"Where're we goin'?"

A woman was talking, but slow and mushed together. Instantly, Charlie's blood ran cold and he rushed toward the woman's voice.

It took a minute, but he finally caught sight of them in the distance, tucked between a couple of larger trucks in the parking lot. It was one of the newer rodeo girls, one Charlie didn't know, and she was tottering back and forth in an obvious drunken sway.

But she wasn't alone.

There was a man with her, one who was obviously trying to coax her deeper into the parking lot, and his steady steps told Charlie that he wasn't nearly as intoxicated, if at all.

It was hard for him to process the deluge of emotions that slammed into him. Rage, anger, shock, fear. He willed himself to move forward, but suddenly his entire body was frozen in the rush that nearly drowned him. Wind roared past his ears and panic rose quickly in his throat. All he could think was *no, no, no, no!*

Before he knew it, he was striding forward, fists balled and arms shaking, but he didn't even get three steps before someone else suddenly appeared.

"Hey there, sugar, I was wondering where you got off to."

Suddenly Daisy darted out from between two cars, her voice bright but with an undercurrent of steel to it.

"Huh?" the girl asked. "I dun... what? I'm thirsty."

"We're just going to go get a drink," the man muttered, his voice low. Threatening.

Charlie took another step forward, but then Daisy was speaking again.

"Aw, sweet of you, but sugar here and I were just in the middle of a conversation. I'd like to get back to that, if you don't mind."

"Hey, she's an adult. If she wants to come with me—"

"But she doesn't, does she?" Daisy snapped so harshly that for a moment even Charlie was surprised. "Do you even know this girl?"

"Sure. We're friends."

"Then prove it."

Charlie heard the guy sputter even from where he was. "What do you mean?"

"Did I stutter? Prove that you know her."

"She doesn't need you babysitting her."

His words rang a bell that Charlie had been avoiding for years. Suddenly the ground fell away from under him and he was dropped back into that time.

"COME ON, Charlie, I got you a drink. You'll like it."

"Why are you always so uptight?"

"Come on, it's not gonna hurt you to cut loose every once in a while."

·　·　·

HE CAME BACK GASPING, his head ringing, and he blinked blearily to see that Daisy was suddenly in the man's face. Or at least as close as she could get to his face considering he had several inches on her.

"Listen here, buddy. I don't recognize you, and I know everyone here. You're not going anywhere with my friend." Charlie couldn't believe how she daringly stared the man down, as if she didn't care he was nearly twice her size. "I'll give you thirty seconds to run out of here as fast as you can before I call over fifty angry and slightly inebriated cowboys to come wail on your sad behind. You got it?"

The man hesitated for a moment, and Daisy jabbed him three times in the chest.

"What about 'get lost' do you have to think about? Beat it!"

That was the last straw, it seemed, because the man did indeed take off, angrily stomping away. Charlie watched, shocked at how the whole thing unfolded, but Daisy was on the move. She wrapped her arm around the drunk girl's shoulders and started to walk her back to the mess hall.

"Come on, sugar. Let's get you some water and some electrolytes, okay? You gotta be careful out here."

Her voice drifted off as Charlie stood there, stunned at everything that had happened. The rodeo had felt so safe. And suddenly that was very much not the case, and the shadows were looming over several parts of his brain. He found himself following a good distance after them until Daisy reached her usual table and set the girl down among her friends. Instantly they were all on the move, someone getting a blanket, someone grabbing a drink, and someone calling for Jeremiah and Marco, the other boss.

That was good. The girl was surrounded by people who would look out for her. Charlie could...

He actually wasn't sure what he could do. His head was spinning, and he felt nauseous. Voices and memories were clamoring around in his mind, shoving him back toward the place he didn't want to go. A place he'd fought to stay away from.

"You're way cooler than I thought, you know that?"

"You've got that squeaky clean image. Makes people want to dirty it up."

No. No. He didn't want to think about that. He'd boarded off all of that and there was no reason to go over it again.

Clearly, the party was a bad idea, and even though it was just barely past ten, Charlie decided it was best to go to bed. If he was asleep, at least he knew the inevitable nightmares would end when he woke up the next day.

7

———————

Daisy

The rodeo was going well, really. Daisy was able to pick up some extra shifts and even landed several free meals, one of them courtesy of the Miller patriarch.

He was a nice enough man, more standoffish than his gregarious son, but still intimidating for her. Daisy wasn't sure why, but older adults always made her nervous. Probably because she knew she wasn't exactly the sort of girl most mothers wanted to see their son bring home. Maybe it was just because she felt awkward around them. Maybe it was because there was always the inevitability where Daisy would turn down a drink and people would get... questiony.

Either way, she said her thanks, ate her fill, then ducked out as soon as she could.

But even with all those blessings, she wasn't quite getting

ahead like she was hoping to. Although she didn't like to admit it to herself, her hopes had been to be able to save up for maybe a deposit on a month-to-month studio. But considering most of the places were looking for first and last months' rent, she'd hardly made a dent in it.

Sure, she'd only be able to stay in the place for three to four months, but still...it would be nice to have a place to call home that wasn't on wheels. And her own bathroom.

...or maybe even some *one* to come home to as well.

Daisy shook her head and focused on getting her riding kit on. She only had three outfits that were really fit for the show, but she did her best to maintain them. Her replacement rhinestones were kept under her first aid kit, and the glue she used to reattach them was always beside her fridge, where the warmth of the appliance kept it from solidifying. She'd learned early on that cold temperatures were not her friend and had practically cried when she'd wasted twelve dollars' worth of product.

But still, even though her financial situation wasn't improving as much as she would like, she was still having a great time. And whenever it was her turn to be a show rider for the barrels, or even a contest, she couldn't believe that she'd managed to nail a job doing something she loved.

It was way better than being a waitress. Or even working in a factory. Granted, if she worked in a factory, she'd probably have her own place and maybe even be able to stable a horse at some farm.

Maybe.

But she wasn't going to give up rodeo life. Not when she loved it so much.

Her call time hit, and Daisy hurried off to the ring. She always liked to get there early and see the four or so riders before her. Usually it was Marco, one of the bosses who would open, then a local rider, then Panama, another local rider, and finally Daisy. Or Scarlet, as most people knew her. It was a pretty heavy responsibility to be the mid-point of the barrel run. That was most likely when the audience's attention was going to flag, and it was up to her to ramp them up for the second half.

And that was part of the challenge Daisy loved.

What was that one phrase? Do what she loved and never work a day in her life? Not entirely accurate, but at least it was fulfilling. Daisy couldn't imagine what it would be like to survive as an office drone.

...she'd probably have better food.

But good food or not, she went out into the arena and did her thing, feeding off the applause like she had before. It was exhilarating, and exhausting, and everything she loved, and once she was out, it was nice to wind down and tend to the horse.

He wasn't hers, and the owners were technically supposed to do it themselves, but most of them were nice enough to let the riders tend to them after a show. It was like a nice comedown and bonding thing, and it certainly helped Daisy bond with the different show animals she had to work with.

Except for Spartacus. He never liked her.

"Hey, Scarlet, you wanna head to the bar after this?"

Daisy looked over her mount she was brushing to see that it was the new girl she'd helped out. Like most of the newer employees, she used Daisy's show name rather than her birth one. She didn't mind though; Scarlet was a pretty cool moniker as far as show names went.

"I'm not sure."

"Aw, come on. It'll be fun and a few of us will feel safer with you there."

Daisy chewed her lip. She'd learned long ago that bars weren't her friend, and they were one of the easiest ways to fall off the wagon. And considering she was still rinsing the mud off her pride from her last tumble, it was too soon to go tempting herself again.

"*Please!*"

Daisy's mind flashed back to that night when she'd first interacted with the girl. It had been some rodeo chaser trying to get her to someplace remote to do who-knew-what, except Daisy had a pretty good idea what it was the man was after. It made her sick. It made her angry. And she knew that—statistically speaking at least—the girls would be safer if she was there.

Even though the towns they were close to were all fairly safe, once people got alcohol in their systems, the story could change so easily.

"Alright, alright, I'll come with you. Just keep your head on yourselves, okay? I don't want me being there to be an excuse to be nitwits about it."

"Oh right, of course. I promise that I won't get that sloppy again."

"Good. You gotta keep your wits about you, you know? You can never play it too safe."

The girl gave an eager nod and ran off. Daisy wondered how she'd ever gotten into a role that felt suspiciously like their rodeo mother when she was only twenty-five, but just shrugged and went with it. It was better than being the eighteen-year-old wild child who spent more of her time blacked out than conscious.

That girl was long since gone and Daisy wasn't too keen on bringing her back.

Good riddance.

As far as bars went, it was actually a pretty great place. Daisy rolled in, about as nervous as one would expect her to be, but then she noticed that there was an entire section of the floor dedicated entirely to line dancing. Several other workers were already having a blast with the locals.

"Now that's what I'm talking about."

It turned out it was pretty easy not to drink when she was learning the dances and laughing her heart out. She wasn't the best, but she wasn't the worst, and it was clear everyone was just genuinely enjoying themselves.

Eventually she needed a breather because she was getting far too sweaty and her boots were starting to hurt her toes. She really needed to spring for those insoles. After getting a water from the bar, she headed over to a different corner that apparently had karaoke.

Daisy was *horrible* at karaoke.

And it was amazing.

Somehow, she ended up singing ABBA with Billy and two other girls while Melinda filmed the entire thing, laughing her head off. It was a good time, a great time, and Daisy didn't even feel the longing to drink even once.

Almost like being a normal person.

And, like a normal person, she did eventually have to use the restroom. Bowing out of their third rendition of *Dancing Queen*, Daisy went to take care of herself, then swung by the bar again to get a glass of soda this time.

"Hey there. You look pretty flushed."

Ugh. She knew that voice.

"That usually happens when someone exerts themselves,

don't cha know?"

Tilting her head, she glanced over to spoiled, rich boy Charlie. Annoyingly enough, he looked handsome in his blue plaid shirt and jeans, because of course he did. Maybe if he wasn't so attractive, he wouldn't irritate her so much. But something about him being killer on the eyes and rich as sin drove her up the wall.

Blargh.

"Oh, I'm aware. I'm just not used to seeing you doing those things."

"I imagine that it's hard to notice such details when you're stuck up in the clouds above all us little people."

It was possibly her most direct insult to him. Daisy didn't like the dude, but she knew better than to antagonize a family that had so much power and influence. It's just that she was having so much fun with her friends, she couldn't help but be extra annoyed that he was there killing her vibes and all of that.

"Is that what you think?"

Oooh, and for the first time, it sounded like she actually got under his skin. Daisy was all ready to get into a verbal spar when suddenly a local girl inserted herself between them.

"Hey there, handsome."

Daisy rolled her eyes, wishing her soda would come faster. The last thing she needed was to see some woman drool all over the guy. He didn't need the ego boost. Gross.

"Sorry but—"

He didn't finish before the woman suddenly *slid onto his lap.* That was certainly a move, and Daisy would have been more impressed if she wasn't so annoyed. Clearly, the woman had a good radar for someone who might buy her a top-shelf drink.

But then Daisy noticed something curious. She expected a cocky sort of grin from the man, and for him to look at her with a smarmy grin or something. But instead, the man stiffened and went pale, his face drawn like the woman had stabbed him.

That... that was weird.

"So what's a girl got to do to get a drink from a good-looking man like you?" the woman practically purred, her hand going up to stroke the Charles dude's thick hair. The man stiffened further and Daisy swore his face turned outright gray.

Wait. That wasn't good. Sure, she didn't like the guy, but he looked *really* uncomfortable.

"Sorry, I've had a long day of work. I just want to have a drink by myself." Now that was just about the last thing Daisy had expected.

"Aw, come on. If you play hard to get, you're gonna hurt a girl's feelings." Her fingers stroked against the man's scalp again and Daisy swore he shivered, and not in the good way. "It ain't right for a handsome guy like you to be all alone here." She leaned in and whispered something in his ear, but all Daisy could hear was something about saving a horse and the word 'cowboy.'

That was it. Sure, they weren't friends, but Daisy wasn't going to sit back and watch someone be harassed when they clearly were upset.

"Hey, the dude said no. Go fulfill your cowboy fantasy somewhere else."

"Excuse me?"

The woman finally twisted to see Daisy, but she was still in Charlie's lap, and that needed to change. She was pretty, sure, with bright blue eyes and blond hair. Daisy wasn't sure why Charlie wasn't interested in the woman, but she didn't need to know why. No meant no and all that jazz. And he clearly didn't want the girl to be sitting in his lap.

"You heard what he said. He's not interested; go take a walk."

The woman huffed up and Daisy prepped herself for some absolute lunacy.

And she wasn't disappointed.

"Listen, I don't know what truck you were dragged under, but you can see yourself out of here."

Daisy stood up, crossing over to the girl. "Do you really want to start something you can't finish, sweetie? I just dealt with horses all day long and they have a much meaner kick than you do in those heels."

"Wait, you're from the rodeo?"

"We both are," she said coolly. "And we like to stick together, so unless you want a whole lotta trouble, it'd be best to back off."

Daisy watched as the woman's eyes shuttled between her and the crowd around her, no doubt wondering who was rodeo folk and who wasn't, but eventually she just huffed.

"Whatever. Who wants to spend time with carnies anyway?"

Finally, she got off Charlie's lap and shoulder-checked Daisy as she sashayed off. But she had all the oomph of a kitten and ended up tripping, barely catching herself on a tall barstool.

"Not a carnie, but nice try."

She huffed again and Daisy glared daggers at her until she hastily exited the bar. Good. People like her didn't deserve to get to enjoy bar life if they couldn't behave themselves. There was an etiquette to it, after all.

"Your cola," the bartender said.

Daisy whirled back around. Grabbing her drink, she took a long, bubbly sip and let out a sigh. "That hits the spot!"

But then her eyes opened, and she saw that Charlie was staring at her, eyes wide and color only now returning to his face.

"You…"

Ugh, no. She didn't like the weight of his stare. It was too much like a spotlight, which was weird because she usually loved being right in the center of it.

"Don't make a big deal of it," she warned, voice low, before hurrying off and returning to karaoke.

After all, she still didn't like the guy.

Even if he was suddenly a whole lot more human.

8

____

Charlie

$\mathcal{D}$aisy was on his mind.

And she shouldn't have been. She didn't belong there. And yet she was. Suddenly she was a lot more prevalent in his life, and he found himself noticing her in his peripherals more often than he ever had before. And all that extra time noticing meant he saw way more of her actions than ever before.

Twice, he saw her help someone out in an unexpected way. Once changing the tire of a local who was stuck in the parking lot, and another time giving a piggyback ride to a rodeo girl who'd twisted her ankle in a gopher hole.

And then there was that scene from the bar that kept replaying in his head ad nauseam.

She told him not to make a big deal of it, and yet his brain constantly made a big deal of it. His skin had been crawling, and he'd been so blindsided by having a woman in his lap that he hadn't known what to do. His first instinct had been to push the woman out of his lap entirely, but he didn't want to get accused of pushing her around or trying to hurt her. His mind had been filled with static, and somehow Daisy had known.

...which was just about the last thing he'd expected.

After all, he was a man, and wasn't it supposed to be a man's fantasy to have a beautiful woman come out of nowhere and flirt with him? And to be honest, Charlie did actually like flirting. It was fun to banter back and forth with an attractive person, to have witty word play and a little tension.

But he didn't like being touched by people he didn't know. He especially didn't like being put on the spot like that either. And somehow... Daisy had known. And she'd basically rode in like a knight in shining armor, chasing the woman away so Charlie could breathe again.

How was his brain not supposed to make a big deal of that?

So, after a week or so had passed and his mind still wouldn't let him let go of it, he decided to approach her.

Easier said than done. The woman was *incredibly* busy. She worked the barrels usually, riding as the mid-show performer, but as their season ramped up, she helped with two of their competitions and also helped with the ticket stands. Whenever she wasn't working, she was either locked in her trailer or partying with her circle of friends. And while Charlie had gotten up the courage to talk to her in private, he didn't really want to address her in a group.

No, he preferred privacy whenever possible. Besides, he felt going up to her in front of her friends would definitely go against her request to not make it a big deal.

Finally, he spotted his chance. Maybe not the best chance,

considering that she was cleaning out the communal bathrooms during the rodeo's version of the weekend, but no one was around to eavesdrop, and he wouldn't be interrupting her relaxing after hours.

"Hey there, Daisy. You need some water?"

She jolted, whirling with her spray bottle raised, but she relaxed when she saw it was him. Which actually was a marked improvement.

"I wouldn't mind that if you're offering."

Charlie tossed her a bottle and she caught it in her off hand. He watched her throat bob as she slugged it down and suddenly, he was acutely aware of the spattering of freckles across her cheeks and shoulders. They weren't normally visible in her riding outfits, but in her pastel blue tank top, they stood out in a gentle smatter of various shades of brown.

"Hey, uh, so I just wanted to say thank you," he started, feeling like he was already on the wrong foot.

"Please don't," she answered quickly, not even looking at him while she tossed the empty bottle into the recycling bin in front of the bathroom. Some rodeos didn't care about such things, but Marco drove them to the bottle returns facility himself for cash that was used for staff parties. As a result, most of the workers were pretty adamant about making sure they went into the proper receptacles.

"Please don't what?"

"Whatever it is you're trying to do. Stop it. You don't need to thank me for anything. A person was being a pest, and I hate that."

"I... I'm just trying to be polite."

"I'm sure you are."

Irritation bristled along Charlie's spine. He was being *nice*.

Why was Daisy being so difficult? She was always so difficult. Between the cursing, the barbs and the general dismissal of his entire being, she was just such a prickly person.

"Why do you always have something against me? If I did something to set you off, I'd love to hear it."

Daisy let out a sigh, rubbing her hands on her shorts. Charlie tried not to follow the motion down, but his eyes still followed the line of her legs anyway. Daisy had great legs, powerful from riding and with more of that gentle dusting of freckles, and it was easy to wonder what it would feel like to pass his hand along her skin. But then he would get that twisting feeling in his stomach and that just made him feel worse.

"You really wanna know, cowboy?"

"I do."

"It's because you get on my nerves. You don't know how the real world works and you're so arrogant about it. You come in here with enough money to bail this entire rodeo out, taking a job that you don't need from someone who's harder up for cash."

Charlie blinked at her. He was arrogant? *How*?

"But like I said, just because I don't like you doesn't mean I'm going to sit there and let someone harass you. It ain't right, okay? Even an annoying rich boy deserves not to have a grabby McGrabberson in his personal space."

There was a lot of insult in there, but Charlie didn't miss the anger aimed at the woman who'd forced herself into his lap. "How did you know that I was uncomfortable? That I didn't want it?"

"What woman doesn't know what it's like to have an unwanted person come onto her? It's a... I guess a look in the eyes, and you had it for sure."

A look in his eyes, huh?

Perhaps some would be insulted, but Charlie was shocked. Every time he explained his aversion to touch by strangers, even pretty female strangers, people always acted like he was crazy, like he was just supposed to be into any womanly attention no matter where it was coming from. But somehow Daisy, a person who didn't even like him, had somehow noticed it from six feet away?

Strange.

"Well, this has been real fun, Charles, but I'm working overtime like normal people have to when they're broke. Thanks for the water, but I'd really like to concentrate on my work now."

Charlie recognized a dismissal when he heard one, even though he still had so many questions. What had he done to make her feel like he was arrogant? When had he ever bragged about his money? And didn't she think it was strange that him, a red-blooded male, had rejected a pretty blond townie for no reason?

But he couldn't ask any of them because she was already marching into the boiling bathroom. The AC was turned off in those on Mondays and Tuesdays—the off days of the rodeo-—so they got to be absolutely miserable. The fact that she'd rather go in there than talk to Charlie and enjoy the breeze, well, it was certainly telling.

"What did I even do?" Charlie asked no one. Everyone liked him. He was charming and cute and witty. His sisters made sure he grew up to respect women and be a generally polite person. What...

Oh well. It wasn't like he could chase her into the bathroom and interrogate her until she told him. He was going to have to let it go and accept that some people weren't meant to like him.

...easier said than done.

9

Daisy

It wasn't enough.

It wasn't enough.

Daisy tried not to cry as she looked at her paycheck. Even with the overtime she'd managed to snag, it wasn't as much as she needed to get back into the black.

What was she going to do?

Pacing her trailer didn't work considering it was basically four steps in any direction, so instead she spun in slight circles before pulling out her phone and dialing a number that she absolutely hated calling.

"Thank you for calling Specter Mobile..."

Daisy went through the prompts until she got to a human, where she found herself having to maintain her composure. She liked to think she was a fairly strong person, but she couldn't keep the warble of embarrassment out of her voice.

"Hi, I'm calling because I'm not going to be able to afford my phone bill this month, and I was wondering if you could do a payment plan for me?"

"Let me look into that for you. Hold one moment, please."

Daisy held, because what else was she supposed to do, tapping her foot as her nerves amped up. She hated that she was so far behind. It felt like a badge of failure branded right into the center of her head, telling everyone around her that she had lost at being an adult and was basically worthless.

After all, who was a certified alcoholic by age eighteen? No one who was a winner, that was for sure.

Be nice, Daisy. She reprimanded herself, trying to remember what her old mentor had taught her. *Self-flagellation is a way the addiction tries to convince you it's not worth fighting. It's always worth fighting. I am worth fighting for. Me. Daisy Dixon. I can do this. I can—*

"I'm sorry, ma'am, but after reviewing your account, you are not eligible for a payment plan."

"Wait, I'm not what?"

"Eligible for a payment plan."

"Why not? Since when was that an eligibility thing?"

"It shows that you've had four payment plans this year, and on the last one, you were three days late on the last payment. You must wait six months before you can do another payment agreement."

"I was late on my last payment because it was a holiday, and the bank didn't process my direct deposit until Monday. The agent I talked to said that was fine."

"That agent was incorrect, ma'am."

Daisy could feel her anger, her embarrassment, and her despair all rising in equal strides. She knew everything would get softer, fuzzier, and a bit more palatable if she just could have one beer, and that temptation in itself just made every emotion that much more intense.

"Look, the only reason I'm behind is because I had this infected tooth and the dental bill ended up being over two grand, and *then* my car broke down. And I *had* to repair it because I literally live in a trailer attached to my truck. I couldn't just leave it in my driveway to deal with later, because I don't have one."

"I'm very sorry to hear that, ma'am, but there's nothing I can do."

Daisy breathed in. Breathed out. Breathed in. Breathed out. Did it a couple more times for extra measure, but none of it seemed to be helping. She wished more than anything she could talk to her mentor, but he was dead, and she hadn't really clicked with anyone since.

Of course, it was hard to click with people when she wasn't actually going to AA meetings.

"What are my options?"

"You can pay your bill here with me, you can set it up for automatic payment, or you can pay it on the due date in… three days."

"But I already explained to you that I don't have the money for the full bill."

"If you do not pay your bill, you have a five-day grace period, and then your phone will be shut off."

"Right. Well, thanks then. You've been a real help."

"Of course, and thank you for—"

Daisy hung up, trying not to cry. She couldn't cry, because once she started, she probably wouldn't stop.

"It's okay. It's just a phone. You can go without it for a week or two and just mooch off some other folk's Wi-Fi for important stuff."

She'd been through worse, after all. Like that time her phone was stolen. And when her truck's passenger side window had been shattered before she had her trailer, so she had to tape it up and shiver under blankets for a month until she could fix it.

But still, that didn't mean that it was easy. Daisy loved her phone. She used it to read herself to sleep at night since digital books didn't take up any room and were free, and to keep track of time, and to make notes for herself.

"At least I can pay my car insurance," Daisy grumbled to herself, keeping her mind occupied by logging in and taking care of that. It wasn't all she wanted to do, but at least paying one bill gave her a modicum of pride.

The pride was short-lived, however, when she saw her meager bank account. And of course, that absence was immediately filled with an uncomfortable sort of emptiness. What was she supposed to do? She was working as much as she could, picking up extra shifts on Monday and Tuesday, skipping meals and trying to snag as many free ones as she could, but she just couldn't get ahead.

It wasn't like she was spending all willy-nilly. And she had never asked for that tooth infection. She'd tried ignoring it as long as she could, but eventually she had to go in, and the dentist said that if she waited much longer there was a chance it could have gone to some sort of valve in her heart.

Ugh.

Daisy needed air.

She rushed out of her trailer, trying to draw in breaths, and the faintest sound of celebration began to drift over to her, but not from the food area. No, it was farther out, and the faintest blush of orange in the distance reminded her that some of the other trailer workers were having a sing-along around a campfire.

Right, Melinda had invited her to that, but there was always so much beer and liquor that Daisy had decided to avoid it. It was the same old, same old with temptation, and although she'd been okay at the bar, that didn't mean she wanted to push her limits.

She knew she should stay away; she *knew*. Feeling worthless and like a failure was her biggest trigger. But she didn't want to be alone, didn't want to have to ruminate in her misery and ineptitude. She wanted to laugh and joke around and be surrounded by people she loved.

She shouldn't though.

She wanted to.

She *shouldn't*.

But what was the point when she always lost anyway?

10

———

Charlie

"Make sure you heat the soup for about three minutes in the microwave and let it cool down, okay?"

"Yes, Clara," Charlie said with a lopsided grin. "I am aware of how to reheat soup."

He could practically hear her roll her eyes over the phone. "Don't sass me. It's easy to accidentally overheat it and scald the whole thing. You don't want to feed your friend nasty, scalded soup, do you?"

"No, I don't. Thank you again for making this."

"No problem. Hopefully it'll help clear his sinuses. Love you!"

"Love you too, sis."

Charlie hung up and finished making his way over to Billy's trailer. The poor guy had come down with a sinus infection something fierce in the middle of the week and still sounded like his nose and head were stuffed full of cotton. Thankfully, when Charlie had messaged Clara asking if she could make one of her delicious comfort soups for exactly that, she'd delivered a case of tall take-out tubs filled to the brim with what looked like chicken n' dumplings, tortilla soup and egg drop soup. Charlie was pretty sure that Clara had specially ordered the tubs for such a situation, and if that wasn't the most Clara thing to do, he didn't know what was.

"Knock-knock, you still alive in there?"

"Nobody says knock-knock in real life," Billy's miserable voice called from inside, footsteps following after a delay. Poor guy, somehow even his walking sounded painful.

"Yeah, well my hands are kinda full so…"

"Full of what?"

That was when the door opened and Charlie wasn't going to lie—he loved the shocked expression on the man's face.

"I don't remember ordering delivery."

"Don't worry, this is a custom donation from my sister Clara. She heard you were under the weather and wanted to help out."

"Clara? Ain't that your sister that Rick took a shine to?" Billy kept his mouth open, apparently not able to breathe at all through his stuffed-up nose.

"Wow, everybody knows about that, huh? That's her."

"Well tell her I said thank you. Do I just stick 'em in the microwave?"

"Actually, Clara's a bit extra, so she stuck a specific bowl in the bottom of this box that apparently is the best for reheating soups without, I dunno, ruining them or something. Maybe I could come in and we could hang out while I reheat some for you?"

"Brother, if you think I'm gonna turn down someone cooking for me when I'm like this, then you have another thing comin'."

"Point taken. Well, let me inside, will you?"

He did just that, backing up and motioning for Charlie to follow him. He and Billy weren't the closest considering that the taller, lankier man worked the ticket stands, sold balloons and did shifts on the food trucks, but he'd never had an unpleasant experience with him. He was a quieter type, but not unpleasantly so, and he played acoustic guitar like God had crafted his fingers specifically for it. As far as Charlie was aware, William Bartherton IV was just a nice, homey sort of dude with a massive nose that apparently lent itself to massive sinus infections.

"So, does your sister always make a week's worth of food for random strangers?"

"Hah, actually, that's kind of her thing. She met her fiancé after she took him a meal for some sort of church program."

"Wow. You Millers are something else, aren't you?"

"Maybe, but you just sit down and let me heat this up. I believe she also put mini bottles of some hot sauce in here in case your congestion is *really* bad. But honestly, her tortilla soup recipe comes from one of the native matriarchs south of town, so it should do the trick."

"Wow, I don't think I could have paid for a delivery service this thorough."

Charlie chuckled and went about doing exactly what he said. It wasn't hard, although he couldn't help a sardonic sort of grin when he found written directions down in the bottom of the box. Oh Clara, she usually wasn't as much of a mother hen as Charity except when it came to her food for sick people.

It didn't take long to reheat a hearty bowl and Charlie handed it off to Billy. It really was one of those high-quality ones because although the soup was steaming, the bowl was only warm to the touch. Charlie remembered once when he was a kid, his mother was sick with the flu and he'd accidentally burned his hands on a hot bowl of chicken noodle soup when he took it out of the microwave. Clara really did think of everything.

"Mind if I chill out here for a few minutes?"

"Sure. I could use the company."

Charlie nodded and sat on the couch built into the wall, watching as Billy tried to blow on the soup but mostly ended up sputtering because of his stuffed nose.

Billy then tried again, taking a long slurp. Charlie didn't get quite the same happiness as Clara did from feeding people, but he did like seeing his friends enjoy themselves. There was a lot of darkness in the world, so he'd take his pieces of sunshine where he could get it.

Billy's face lit up, his ginger brows going all the way up to his hairline, and he eagerly took three more gulps. His face flushed pink, and suddenly he was grabbing a tissue from beside his bed and blowing his nose like a foghorn.

"Whew!" he gasped, looking to Charlie like he was an angel. "I can *breathe*. Actually *breathe*."

"You're welcome."

"Your sister is amazing."

"Yeah, she is."

"You're totally gloating over there."

"Not gloating, but I do admit I'm glad to help you feel better. But I realize that I forgot to give you a spoon. You want one?"

"Nah. I'm slugging this. I feel like a new man already. What did she put in this stuff?!"

"Clara will love to hear that. She gets a real kick out of people enjoying her food."

He took another long, noisy slurp, and it was pretty gratifying. Maybe Charlie should try to cook something for the workers the next Monday-Tuesday break.

Eh... maybe not. He didn't have the same magic to his food that Clara did. He was more than capable of getting by, but there was a joy she had that she seemed to infuse right into the food itself.

Not physically possible, and yet... that was the only way that Charlie could describe it.

"Man, if your sister wasn't happily taken, I might fight Rick for her attention."

Charlie could only chuckle at that, imagining two of the most wholesome thirty-something men he knew in a court-off for Clara.

"Ah, sorry, man, I didn't mean to talk about your sister like that in front of you."

"Don't worry, you were being respectful. If you weren't, well, the soup would be in your lap. Clara is amazing, as are Charity, Cassidy and Cici. I can't blame people for recognizing that." Charlie thought a minute.

"Huh, you're a pretty chill guy, you know that? I don't have any sisters, but I know a lot of my friends growing up got weirdly protective of them. And not in the healthy way."

Charlie nodded. "I know what you mean. It's a hard line to walk, being a brother. You want to protect them from the whole world. You want to be responsible for them. But you also have to realize that they're people and grown women, and you have to respect that."

Charlie smiled and then continued. "I guess it's easier for me to get because I'm the second youngest, so they were the ones teaching me growing up, but still... I think it's a valuable lesson for anyone who's a brother."

"Wait, your sisters were teaching you that? I would have thought that was something your mother might do."

Charlie pressed his lips together in a thin line. He'd long since come to terms with the loss of his mother, but when she came up out of nowhere, it blindsided him sometimes. Half of him thought he and Cici had it easier because they were younger when Mama Miller passed. They hadn't had her in their lives for as long, and they couldn't really comprehend that she was gone and had longer to digest that reality. But sometimes, he felt like they'd been cheated out of the years with her that his eldest siblings had.

"She passed when I was young."

"Oh, man, I'm sorry. I think I remember vaguely hearing something about that."

"It's alright. It's just a fact of my life. But as you can imagine, it was real hard on my Papa, so my sisters covered a lot of gaps that he couldn't, since he was mourning the love of his life."

"You've been through it, haven't you?" Billy paused to drink some more soup. "No wonder you're so easygoing."

"We've all had our trials."

"Yeah, but—"

Charlie was just about ready for the conversation to be over when a sudden banging at the door cut Billy off. Thank goodness.

"I'll get that," he offered, already on his feet.

Subtly heaving a sigh of relief, Charlie rushed over and threw it open. He wasn't sure who or what he was expecting, but it wasn't Daisy Dixon, who was swaying slightly on her feet.

"Wait..." she slurred, her red eyes focusing on him with startling acuity considering how much her body language conveyed that she was absolutely sloshed. "This is supposed to be Billy's place. Where's Billy?"

"Calm down. He's sick, remember?"

"I know. That's why I came by. I wanted to make sure he was alright. He has to drink lots of... of water. I don't want him to get dehydrated. That's *bad*."

Well, she wasn't wrong.

"I brought him some homemade soup from my sister and made sure he's okay."

"Oh, did you? That's so nice. You're so nice. It's annoying."

Wait, she thought he was nice? No, that had to be the alcohol talking. The smell of it made Charlie's skin crawl, and he was tempted to just leave her swaying there.

"Well, if he's okay, I should... I should let him rest, right? Yeah. Rest is good." She looked at him sharply. "Is he resting?"

"Yeah. He's resting."

"Oh, okay then. I'll go home then."

Charlie watched her take a couple of steps but then stop. She stood there a moment, then turned in the opposite direction, but then stopped again.

"Where did I park? Do you know?"

Oh dear.

"Hold on, you stay there."

"But I'm supposed to go home. It's not safe to be out alone when you're drunk, don't you know?"

Oh, Charlie knew.

"Just stay there. I'll be right out. I promise."

She shot him such an open, vulnerable look that for a moment Charlie forgot what he was even supposed to be doing. "Pinky promise?"

"Sure. Just don't move."

"Kaykay."

Charlie had no idea what was going on, but he spun on his heel and marched back into the trailer. "Daisy's outside. I'm going to walk her to her trailer so she doesn't have to be alone."

"Does she have one of her migraines again? I thought she hadn't gotten one in a while."

Migraines, huh? "Yeah, something like that. I'll stop by later, okay?"

"Sure. With these soups I feel like a new man."

"Make sure you stay hydrated and rest."

"Yeah, point taken. Tell Daisy I said feel better."

"She says the same to you."

What a strange world to be in. With a lazy salute, Charlie hurried out, where Daisy was standing in the exact same place, her head tilted toward the sky.

"It's so beautiful," she said, apparently hearing him as he approached her. "Sometimes I feel like I'm so busy that I don't ever get to look up. That's sad, isn't it?"

What on earth was going on?

"That's very sad. Now come on, let's go."

"Wait, how do you know where I live?"

"I don't, but you have your keys on you, don't you?"

Her eyes widened again, and she looked so pleased that it was easy to forget that she'd just called him arrogant the week earlier. "Wow, I do. You're so smart! They're in my pocket."

She pulled them out and before Charlie could tell her to beep her horn instead of setting off the alarm, she hit the red button and a shrill sound filled the lot.

"There it is."

"Great. But why don't you turn that off, so we don't disturb other people."

"Oh *geez,* you're so smart. Like really smart. How did you get to be so smart?"

Charlie didn't answer, that same skin-crawly feeling all over him. He had nothing against people enjoying their drink of choice, but he couldn't help that drunk people always made him uncomfortable.

Actually, maybe uncomfortable wasn't the right word for it. But he didn't have time to find the right word for it, because he was busy trying to lead Daisy toward where the alarm sound had come from without touching her.

Eventually, they rounded one of the older, bigger RVs and came to a broken-down, rusted truck with the tiniest little tin trailer he'd ever seen. It seemed barely bigger than a bed from the outside and looked like it might fall apart any moment.

"Alright, you're home."

"I am. It's my *home.* She goes with me everywhere." She giggled and staggered forward, lifting her hand with her keys only to drop them on the ground. "Whoops. Let me handle that."

She bent down, picking the set up, only to drop them again after she straightened.

"Gosh, they're slippery."

"Nevermind, I got it."

Grabbing them, Charlie quickly unlocked the door and held it open for Daisy. But when he looked back, she was already tottering off, and he reached out on instinct.

"You want to go inside, don't you?"

"Hmmm?"

Sighing, Charlie gently coaxed her into the trailer. Part of him was pretty uncomfortable going into a small, enclosed space with someone who was inebriated. His heart began to pound and sweat beaded on his forehead. He had to concentrate very hard not to push her away and race out, but he just wanted Daisy to be in her home where she could pass out and not stumble into trouble.

Finally, he got her in, and finally she pushed past him to flop face-first on her bed. Although bed was an awfully generous term for it. It was a thin, barely there mattress directly on the floor.

"Thank you, you can... you can go now."

"Yeah, I'll uh... see you later."

"Duh, we work together, Charlie boy."

Charlie might have rolled his eyes if he wasn't so preoccupied by the sight around him. He had always been raised to understand that people came from all different walks of life and financial situations, but he'd never been in direct contact with a situation so...

Dire.

Besides the mattress there was only a small, beat-up-looking mini-fridge, a microwave and a laundry basket. There was no bathroom, no sink, no dresser, no TV. Not a single one of the amenities that were just a matter of course in his RV.

"Hey, don't do that?"

"Do what?" Charlie asked, nearly jumping. Thankfully, he didn't, because he probably would have hit his head on the buckling ceiling.

"You're judging me. I can feel it."

"I'm not judging you."

"Yes, you are—oh *no!*"

Suddenly, she was up and racing out of the door again, and

Charlie followed after her only to find her tossing her cookies just behind her truck.

"Go away."

Or at least that was what Charlie assumed she said. It was hard to hear it over her retching. Once more, part of him wanted to recoil, but instead he moved forward and held her hair back until she was done.

"You must think I'm pathetic," she murmured when she was done, leaning heavily against him.

"I don't think anything. Let's just get some water in you and get you to bed, okay?"

"Mm... kay."

She was quieter after that, and Charlie led her back inside. Thankfully, she laid on the bed herself, so he didn't have to tuck her in or anything like that. All he had to do was get her a bottle of water, move her trash can over in case she got sick, and that was that.

"This your first time seeing someone fall off the wagon?" she slurred, looking at him with an absolutely miserable eye. Maybe it was that expression that gave him pause. His panic was ramping up further, telling him he was in danger, but she just looked so... lost.

"What was that?"

"Nothing... thanks, Charlie."

Charlie didn't know what to say, but then a gentle snore told him he didn't have to worry about it. With one last look around at the meager surroundings, Charlie exited.

...what a weird day.

Half-dazed, Charlie headed back to Billy's. It was nice to get fresh air without the smell of alcohol wafting from Daisy.

But as he walked, he couldn't get her out of his head again.

From her tiny little home to the run-down condition of everything she owned, to how utterly unhappy she looked as she laid limp on her mattress.

He knocked and Billy let him in.

"Hey friend, how'd it go?" Billy asked. "You get Daisy home safe like the knight in shining armor you are?"

"It went. Do you know what falling off the wagon means?"

"It means—wait, was Daisy drunk?"

Something about the shocked way the man said it made Charlie realize that maybe the situation was much more serious than he thought. "Yeah. She was pretty far gone."

A string of curses passed out of Billy's mouth, leaving Charlie wondering if he was missing something. "That's the second time since she's come back. That's really not good."

"Wait, what's not good? She's a grown adult." Sure, Charlie wasn't fond of people getting drunk around him, but he also understood that adults were going to do what adults wanted to do as long as they weren't hurting other people.

"Yeah, she is, and also a recovering alcoholic. She had such a good streak going before." Then Billy's eyes went even wider. "I'm not supposed to tell you that. It's private. Please, don't let word get out. I gotta go talk to Melinda. Do you mind if I take a raincheck on this hangout?"

"No problem," Charlie murmured, his mind already taking off without him.

Daisy was an alcoholic? Now that he thought about it, he never saw her with a beer in her hands, and at the bar she'd only been ordering soda.

That... huh.

Charlie saw himself out, Billy already hurrying away, leaving him to think about the whole situation. As confusing as it was, the one thing he was certain of was that it was all very... sad.

11

Daisy

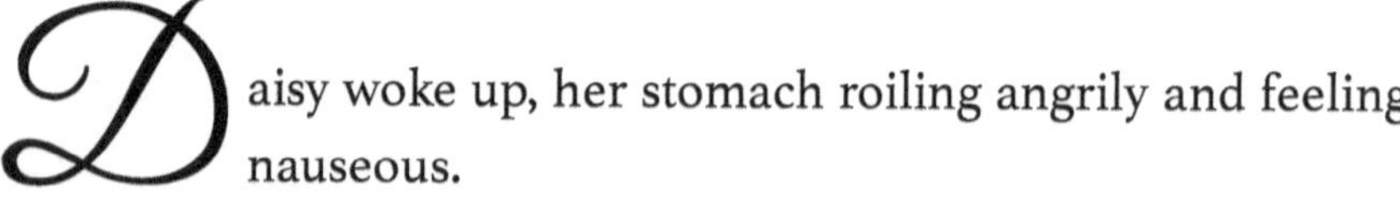aisy woke up, her stomach roiling angrily and feeling nauseous.

For a moment, she couldn't remember what happened. Did she have the flu? Eat something that had disagreed with her? Did she—

Oh.

It hit her in an embarrassing rush of clarity and Daisy let out a tiny, defeated groan. She'd gotten drunk again. Like *really* drunk. She couldn't remember much, which was even worse. Black out Daisy was... well, she was a character.

Depressed, Daisy slowly picked herself out of bed. Her entire body hurt and her head felt like it was expanding then shrinking while an elephant slowly stepped on it. It took her several minutes, but eventually she found her wallet and pulled out her last milestone token from AA.

"...what a waste," she murmured to herself, turning the token over and over again in her fingers. She hadn't gone in ages because she was so busy working extra shifts. Besides, with gas being expensive and her trying to make her junker last as long as she could, she couldn't justify the repeated trips.

Before, she would have just called her mentor and talked to him on the phone whenever she felt like she was slipping, but he was gone now, and she was all alone.

What was she supposed to do? She knew technically she should just start over—that was how it went when one fell off the wagon—but hadn't done two stumbles one right after the other in a while. How did she pick up after that? Was there even a point?

She could feel herself beginning to spiral, the floor slipping out from under her, and it was oh so tempting to find another beer so she could forget for a little while. Drunk Daisy had no bills, didn't have to worry about her phone getting shut off.

Drunk Daisy was—

A knock sounded on the door and the sound ricocheted around in her head. She barely managed to get a handle on herself before answering it, her vision blurry.

She expected it to be one of her friends. Maybe Melinda with coffee or Rose with breakfast. But instead, it was none other than Charlie Miller.

...what?

"Hello?" she murmured, her own voice sounding absolutely wrecked even to herself.

"I've got some hangover tea for you and some food, if you're interested," he said cautiously, lifting a plastic bag that looked like it was pretty full.

"Hangover tea?" It took her a beat to realize the more pressing issue. "Wait, how do you know where I live? Or that I'm hung over?"

"I walked you home yesterday afternoon. You were in kind of a bad way."

Daisy wanted to deny it, but as the man spoke, the memories came back in a hazy sort of wave.

"I am *so* sorry. I'm not usually—"

"It's okay," he interrupted, and goodness if he didn't sound genuine. "Life happens sometimes. May I come in?"

If it were any other instance, Daisy would have said no. She was very protective of, and totally embarrassed by, her space and didn't let just anyone in. But as more memories began to trickle into the back of her head, she felt obligated to.

Which was pretty weird for her.

But, to her surprise, Charlie didn't say anything about the surroundings as he entered. Instead, he pulled a thermos out of his bag and handed it to her, then went about putting a plate in the microwave. No comment about her tall pile of dirty clothes in the hamper, no mention of how they were more crowded than sardines. He just looked like he was concentrating on the meal.

"You just happened to have this tea on hand?" Daisy asked curiously, popping off the lid. She was surprised when a delicious scent wafted up from it, something nutty and maybe even a touch floral. Tentatively, she took a sip and it tasted just as good as it smelled.

Huh, that was nice.

"No, it was my sister. I drove home last night and asked my sister to whip up a batch."

"You told your sister about me?" Daisy felt her gut churn at the idea of more people finding out what a mess she'd been.

"No. I figured you didn't want it made out to be a big deal. I just told her that it was for a lot of the crew."

"Thank you." She hadn't expected that kind of discretion from him. In all honestly, she didn't expect anything that had happened since she woke up.

"No problem."

Quiet settled between them until the microwave dinged, and then he was handing her a plate that was surprisingly cool to the touch considering how much the food was steaming. Daisy took it, sitting down on the edge of her mattress. When she'd first woken up, she was way too nauseous to even think of eating, but when the food was in front of her, she wondered if she'd ever been so hungry in her life.

And it was *delicious.*

Warm, salty, full of grease but not grossly so. It was the perfect hangover food to go with the sharp, aromatic tea.

"So what, are you on some sort of healing mission to help random drunks get clean?"

Yikes, that sounded so defensive. Daisy hadn't meant for it to come out that way, but she couldn't understand why he was there. He wasn't anything like she expected.

"No, nothing like that," he said calmly, moving to stand by her door. "But I am willing to drive you to AA meetings if you want."

Daisy stopped hastily shoving food into her mouth and looked at the man. Really looked at him. His posture was relaxed. His expression was serious, but not judging.

Strange, strange and stranger.

"Who told?"

"You did," he answered with a shrug. "You asked me if I ever saw anyone fall off the wagon."

Although her headache was easing with every slug of the tea, it throbbed in embarrassment at that.

"Wow, I really am my own worst enemy." More of Drunk Daisy's shenanigans. That girl couldn't keep a secret for her life, and it had certainly gotten Sober Daisy into a lot of trouble once the dust cleared.

"I realize we're not exactly close, but I don't mind. I have to go into the city plenty, and sometimes it's just nice to be on the open road."

Daisy squinted at the man, trying to puzzle out if it was a trick or something of that sort. People didn't offer to waste hours of their life and valuable gas in their car just to drive a pathetic rodeo drunk to their AA meetings.

Then again... not everyone was a millionaire.

Daisy thought back to something her mentor said, about sometimes accepting a helping hand even if that hand doesn't make sense, and that pride needed to take a back seat every so often. Well, she couldn't think of a more apt situation for either of those two lessons, so she swallowed thickly and tried to sound like an adult who at least had their life somewhat together when she answered.

"Thank you. I would be appreciative of that. I usually go every other week or so, but given uh... given my current state, I wouldn't mind going to the one tonight."

Strangely enough, Charlie seemed to perk up at that. "There's one tonight?"

"They're usually Tuesdays, Thursdays, Fridays and Saturdays. Different people run different ones depending on what town we drive to, but I'm familiar with most of them from the circuit."

"Alright then. You finish up your food and tea, maybe take a shower. I'm going to go take a nap and then I'll be back around."

"Five would be best, if we want to get there at a good time."

"Alright. Five it is."

He gave her a nod and then walked out, leaving Daisy to wonder if she'd finally drank too much and had started hallucinating things that absolutely could not happen.

"This is it?"

"Uh-huh," Daisy said, already unbuckling herself and hopping out the door. She'd asked Charlie to take her to Marley's meeting, which was in a mid-sized town about forty-five minutes away from the rodeo. It was held inside the run-down American Legion, tucked back among the corn fields that always smelled vaguely of cow manure. "Thanks for driving me here."

"Don't mention it. You go get what you need."

Daisy nodded, still not sure what to say or do. The drive had been so awkward with neither of them saying anything, just low tunes playing over the radio. But what was she supposed to say? The last time she'd talked to the guy she'd called him arrogant and spoiled. Not exactly a normal jump-off for him turning into a sort of free ride-sharing service for her.

And where was the judgment?

If there was one thing Daisy prided herself on socially, it was that she saw things that other people didn't. She saw the way that Charlie would flinch away from some of the rodeo girls, like he was afraid that they would contaminate him. She didn't miss the subtle curl of his lip when someone offered him free booze. He never attended parties, never tried to make himself a part of the family. And when people vented about their financial problems, he would just say nothing and stand there. She wasn't kidding when she said the guy could probably fix everyone's issues and not even notice the dent in his wallet. The guy was loaded big time. Multi-millionaire style.

But when she thought about it, he'd flinched away from the woman at the bar too. And not because he looked disgusted by her, but because he looked downright terrified. Maybe... maybe she'd misread him?

If so, wow, she was a real cad.

But she could worry about that later. First thing to worry about was going to her actual meeting; second was finding a ride back home. That wasn't exactly going to be easy, but still, Charlie had done her a solid by motivating her to get out of her trailer and actually do something.

Almost as soon as she was in the door, she was enveloped in a hug. "Hey there, Daisy, I haven't seen you in a while. I thought you'd left me for Jerry's meetings."

"Well, he does bring a dozen more cream-filled donuts than you do," Daisy shot back, returning the hug with relief. Every time she skipped out on AA for a while, whenever she came back, she would wonder why she'd avoided it so much in the first place.

"But does he make sure there are fresh fruit and vegetable trays for a rich and varied snack selection?" Marley asked, letting go and stepping away.

"You may have a point there."

"It's good to see you back, hun."

"It's good to be back."

And Daisy meant it. Marley was an older, portly woman with

electric pink hair and a smile about a mile wide. She was warm, friendly and understanding. It was crazy to know her story, how she'd been a mean and abusive drunk, and it took her youngest daughter asking why Marley hated her to convince her to get sober. But it just went to show what alcohol did to some people. Daisy wished she was normal, wished she was one of those people who could be responsible and just enjoy a leisurely beverage. She wasn't.

But at least in AA she wasn't alone.

Charlie had been much more punctual than she had expected him to be, so she was able to chitchat with several other people she hadn't even realized she'd missed before the meeting started. And then, it was time for things to begin. The meeting was exactly what Daisy needed.

She talked about falling off the wagon. She talked about her money troubles and how her dentist bill setting her so far into the hole was really triggering her desire to self-soothe with alcohol. And everyone around her understood. They listened. They didn't judge. They'd all been there—but more importantly—they'd all gotten out to the other side and that's what gave Daisy hope.

And she really, desperately needed hope.

Funny, how most things in her life were so expensive they were usually out of her reach, and yet it was hope that sometimes seemed the most impossible to have. It would float by her occasionally, shimmering and oh so tantalizing, but every time she reached out for it, it would just slip through her fingers like a dream she was never meant to hold.

She was so busy riding the high of the meeting that she almost forgot that she needed to find a ride back to the rodeo.

But just as she was starting to ask around, Marley was approaching her again.

"Hey, lovey, I was just wondering..."

Here we go.

"Ever since Terrance passed, bless his soul, I notice you've been coming less and less. Have you found another mentor?"

"No, I haven't."

Marley got that look on her face which could only be described as motherly. "And why haven't you, Miss Daisy Dixon?"

Daisy shrugged, not really wanting to get into it. How could she succinctly say that filling his spot felt like forgetting him? He'd been with her for three years and had led her through some of the darkest times of her life. He'd never judged her, had always had wise words and an understanding heart. He was the father she never had.

And he was gone.

"I know that Terrance was an incredible man, and that no one can fill his shoes, but you need an ally. Someone to check in with and have your back. We're here for you, and you know that."

"I'll try."

"That's all we can ask. And you know you can always call me, right?"

"Of course I do, Marley."

And that was absolutely true. Daisy knew Marley would help her out of any jam or provide words of advice, but she just didn't have the same connection to the older lady that she did to Terrance.

Daisy didn't know if she could trust another full-grown adult like she had him. He truly was a one-of-a-kind man.

"Alright, you have a good night now. I've got to hurry home."

She headed off and Daisy realized that their conversation had lasted just long enough for pretty much everyone she knew to have left as well.

Shoot. She needed a ride!

Hurrying outside, Daisy pulled her phone out, wondering if she would be the worst person in the world if she asked Melinda or Billy for a ride. But she barely even got her contact list out when she realized that a familiar Jeep was waiting there for her.

"Oh, you're still here," Daisy said, eyes going wide.

He was leaning against the back of his Jeep, watching some sort of video on his phone. He had that sort of casual, unaffected cool that Daisy had never been able to master, and for a moment she was struck by the image of him.

Goodness, he was unfairly attractive.

"Was I supposed to go somewhere else?"

"You offered a ride here but never said anything about a ride back, so I just assumed I'd be on my own. I never expected you to wait."

"Ah, it was no trouble, not really."

"The meeting lasted over an hour, seems like a long time to wait."

But he just shrugged. "I've got time to kill."

Huh.

Daisy stood there a moment, trying to catch up to her rapidly shifting perspective of the man before her. Who drove someone who didn't even like them almost an hour away then stuck around for another hour waiting for them.

"Since you're here, may I have a ride back?"

"Of course. I think that's a good solution."

"You're not wrong there."

He nodded and went around to open the door on the passenger side for her. Daisy slid into the seat, her head still spinning between all the different emotions and responsibilities she was trying to balance.

"Let's head home," Charlie said with a warm smile that Daisy didn't feel she deserved before they hit the road again.

12

———

Charlie

Time passed, shows happened, contests were successes and failures, and perhaps most importantly to Charlie, the frost between him and Daisy truly began to fade.

She was still standoffish, jumpy even, but he understood. It was clear that Daisy was private about her struggle with alcoholism, and she hadn't planned on Charlie finding out about it. She'd handled it pretty well, though, and came to Charlie multiple times to ask him to drive her to a meeting.

He was proud of her, if that made sense. No one in his family really struggled with addiction, but that didn't mean he was blind to it. Society could be real cruel to people fighting their vices, which didn't really make sense considering it was a disease. Charlie was well aware that if word got out that Daisy was in recovery, it could seriously hamper many things in her life, from losing her off-season job to discrimination in her medical care.

"Hey, you need to stop staring at Scarlet, or Miss Sugar in front of you is going to get jealous."

Charlie blinked, bringing himself back to reality before his eyes flicked to Tito. "Pardon me?"

"You're staring at that rider instead of brushing the pretty girl in front of you. If you're not careful, she might stomp on your toes."

"Nah, Miss Sugar wouldn't do that to me. Would you, girl?" Charlie asked the horse that he was tending to. Part of his rotating schedule meant he got to do all sorts of tasks, and he was pretty thrilled that the current week's printout had him tending to most of the mounts in the morning and evening.

Miss Sugar, however, just let out a wuffle and pressed into the brush. Okay, maybe he should concentrate on the horse. She did work awful hard and was wonderful with children.

"But seriously, you two a thing yet? Benny said he saw you driving off together a couple nights back."

Oh, shoot.

"No, we're not a thing."

"Ah, I see. Just some casual tension relief then."

Charlie stopped brushing again. He knew what Tito was implying, and for some reason it upset him. Daisy was a flirty woman, charismatic and charming, but that didn't mean that she was sleeping around with any man whose care she was in. And even if she was, it wasn't anybody's business but hers and her partners.

"Cut it out, man. Be respectful."

"I'm not being disrespectful. She's hot and an adult, no shame in that."

"You don't need to be talking about the hypothetical sex lives of your coworkers," Charlie heard himself snap. "It's weird and invasive."

"Whoa, man, chill. I literally didn't mean anything by it. It's just... you've never been much of one for the ladies. Just wanted to congratulate you for, you know, expanding your horizons."

"Nothing is expanding, Tito. Maybe you're the one who should pay attention to Thunderflanks before he kicks you."

"Alright, alright. Touchy subject. I got it."

But even when Tito quieted down, his words lingered around Charlie's mind. Sure, Charlie didn't date around, didn't court, because he had all he needed on the ranch. Papa, his sisters, the animals and everything else.

Then again, with Charity, Cass, and Clara all finding love from people who were strangers, maybe... maybe something like that would be possible for him.

Because Charlie was a young man just as much as everyone else. Sometimes he wondered what it would be like to kiss someone, to hold someone, to want to curl up on the couch while it was raining and watch a good movie.

But when he thought about actually being that physically close to someone, of having to trust a stranger when he was tired and vulnerable, that desire would usually shrivel up like a dead plant. He hated that. He hated that something was broken inside of him, yet it was something he'd learned to live with. He didn't need anything off the ranch.

But lately, when he looked at Daisy, he wondered if having connections outside of the ranch would be so bad. She was broken too, in her own way. She knew what it was like to have a secret she found shameful, one that she didn't want anyone to know. It would be nice to be close to someone who understood him.

Too bad that was never going to happen. Even if Charlie somehow got over the skin-crawling feeling he got every time someone got too close, Daisy wouldn't be interested in someone like him. She was an attractive person and basically a rodeo star with dozens of people pining after her. She could get affection, admiration and plenty of laughter. Why would she want to deal with a homebody who wasn't even sure if he could hug her?

Ugh.

So, Charlie tried to shove those thoughts out of his mind. He worked, had fun, and grew even closer with his fellow rodeo employees. He drove Daisy to one more AA meeting, and he drove back home on Sunday night rather than sticking around for another worker bonfire and party. He was exhausted, through and through, and he was more than ready to just flop over in his room.

Of course, that all came to a halt when he walked in on what was absolutely a romantic, candlelit dinner between Papa and the Librarian.

"Oh, Charlie! We didn't expect you back this week."

Papa was already on his feet, smoothing down his tie—he was wearing a *tie!*—and Charlie couldn't fight the wide grin that spread across his features.

"Hey there, Papa, and who is this lovely lady here?"

The Librarian—he really should commit to memorizing her name if Papa was bringing her home for candlelit dinners—laughed, a cute flush going to her wizened face. She really had a lovely energy to her. No wonder Savannah was such a big fan.

"This is Miss Edalira. You've met before."

"You're right," Charlie said, giving a bow to the older woman.

"Forgive me. I'm thoroughly exhausted. Please, don't interrupt your meal on my behalf."

"*Charlie*," Papa whispered, sounding embarrassed which was an absolutely wild thing to hear from his dad.

"I'm going. Goodnight, Papa."

Charlie opened his arms for a hug, because hugs from his family never made his skin crawl like a stranger's could, but he took the chance to whisper in his father's ear.

"I'm proud of you."

It was a simple phrase, uttered quietly, but when Charlie pulled away, he could see a slight redness to his father's eyes. Oh, Papa, he worked so hard for everyone. Charlie was ecstatic to see that his dad was finally willing to pursue something that made him happy.

It also made Charlie wonder if he could ever move past the horror that always seemed to be lurking inside of him.

Probably not.

"Thank you, son."

Papa gave him two claps on the back and Charlie headed off to his room, humming happily to himself. Maybe he didn't need anything other than what was on the Miller lands, but he was glad that Papa had finally reached out for himself.

SLEEPING AT HOME WAS REFRESHING, and sticking around all of Tuesday for his regular chores and dinner with his family had Charlie's internal battery all the way refilled. He liked waking up to find Clara in the kitchen, straining the milk she'd gotten from the goats. He missed the way Charity would zombie-walk her way in after him and go straight to the coffee that Clara had already brewed. He missed how Cici would come bounding in about an hour later and gratefully shove whatever Clara or Papa had cooked into her mouth, while Cass would roll in with much less pep in her step. It felt good to be a part of something. To be loved and provided for.

But he couldn't help but wonder if there was anyone to do that for Daisy.

A completely ridiculous thought, of course. He didn't know a single thing about Daisy's home life. Her parents, her siblings, her pets, nothing. He only knew about her rodeo life and show-stopping persona.

However, when Wednesday rolled around, he found himself wondering that as soon as he saw her talking to one of the horses. She looked well enough, but had she been okay over the rodeo-weekend? Had she fallen off the wagon again? Had she been eating? Hydrating properly?

He almost thought about approaching her and asking, but he felt like that wasn't a level of familiarity they were at yet. She thought he was arrogant, right? Trying to mother her like she was a baby who couldn't take care of herself certainly wouldn't help that.

But still... he worried.

So yeah, maybe he called a local restaurant and ordered enough food for the whole crew one night. Maybe he also tucked forty dollars into the pocket of a pair of jeans in her laundry basket when she was distracted trying to give him back the thermos and plate that had come with Clara's hangover food. Maybe he was entirely far too interested in her health, but there was no stopping him now. There apparently was a real busybody gene in the Miller line, and Charlie recognized that he was already invested beyond the point of denying it.

"Hey, you skipped out on the weekend bonfire last week," Raph said, tossing Charlie one of those sugary, bottled coffees that were more caramel than caffeine. "You coming tonight?"

"Aw, did you miss me, Raph?"

"Like ya miss a bad cold."

"You don't have to sweet-talk me. I'll be there."

"Awesome. Hey, do you know that Ted guy who just joined last year?"

"He's the college kid, right? Sophomore now or something? Dark hair?"

"That's him. Well, apparently he's some sort of big deal college football guy and he's bringing a gaggle of cheerleaders from the local college."

Charlie stiffened. "Oh."

"Come on, why do you look terrified? Who doesn't love college cheerleaders?"

"Just leave it alone, Raph."

"Man, I remember how you had all the ladies falling over you in high school. You used to make out with Tina, Bella, Sabine *and* Christy under the bleachers on set days of the week. What happened? You act like you're scared of women now."

"I said leave it alone, Raph."

"Look, if you're gay, that's chill, man. I don't care. But you don't seem—"

"*Raph!*"

It was the first time that Charlie had ever raised his voice like that with his friend, and he felt several people stare in his direction. That was just about the last thing he wanted, so he rubbed at the back of his neck. "Look, I just... I like my space, okay? I need you to not poke at it."

Anybody else probably would have gotten offended, maybe

even yelled back at him. But Raph was Charlie's longest friend so the man just sighed.

"I'm sorry, Charlie. I didn't mean to push you. I'm just worried about you, okay? I've known you for a long time and I can't help but feel like something's wrong."

Charlie's mind was clamoring to say something, to explain about the skin crawling and the stomach heaving and the rushing panic that surged up inside of him every time a girl started coming on to him. But instead, he just shrugged. "People change sometimes, okay?"

"Okay, if that's what you want to leave it at, then that's what we'll leave it at. I'm gonna go get us some lunch, then I'm gonna come back and we'll move on. Sound good?"

"Sounds good."

"Alright, man. You know you're my brother, right, Bible-boy?"

"Yeah, brothers."

Raph gave a nod and headed off, giving Charlie time to breathe. He was embarrassed out of his mind and once again wondered why he couldn't be normal. Why the thought of cheer-leaders coming made him queasy instead of interested or excited. He wished...

He wished a lot of things.

But, true to his word, he did roll up to the bonfire about half an hour after it started, bringing a cooler full of franks and burgers to cook.

It was Rick who approached him first, wide grin across his face and cheeks flushed. "Glad you joined us. We missed you last week."

"Did you miss me, or the chance to ask about my sister?"

"*Nah*, it sounds like Miss Clara is in good hands. I know

better than to bark up a tree I'm not needed at." Rick slung an arm around his shoulder.

Charlie *hated* when people did that without warning, but he didn't feel the need to snap at his friend. Instead, he just ducked under the arm and took a step away.

Rick continued. "Believe it or not, we missed you. You have some great stories. I don't know anyone else who has three goats dedicated to world domination."

That actually surprised Charlie, and he barked out a sharp laugh. "I can't believe you remembered that. Just so you know, Thorin, Arwen and Eowyn have all calmed down. Clara's real good with animals."

Rick let out a sigh. "Yeah, you've mentioned that before. Maybe one day I'll meet a nice lady who'll wanna have a goat herd with me. Maybe some cows. And a *horse*. A really *big* horse."

It was clear that Rick was tipsy, but he was so earnest that Charlie didn't entirely mind. "Dream big, Rick. You're a good guy. You'll find your farm girl if you keep looking for her."

"She's out there for me, I know it. But in the meantime, let's see what you got in that cooler of yours. You always bring the best chow."

"Well, I certainly hope I don't disappoint."

It didn't take long for the cooler to attract other attention, and soon Charlie found himself surrounded by his fellow workers. Smiling faces, all of them, and someone hauled over a grill. Raph approached just when the coals started to catch, and the relieved grin on his face warmed Charlie's chest. Raph could be intrusive sometimes, but he knew his friend really did care about him. He had Charlie's back, even if he didn't understand it.

Too bad he'd been sick when—

"Hey, who started the party without us?"

Charlie recognized that voice and looked over his shoulder to see none other than Ted approaching with three pretty young women with him. Charlie was aware that he was likely only four or five years older than the cheerleaders, but they all just looked so *young* to him.

In fact, they looked like—

"That's what happens when you show up two hours after we get started," someone said wryly. Jeremiah maybe?

"Okay, fair, but I think you'll excuse me since I was out getting some brewskis." He gestured to the cart he was pulling behind him, and Charlie saw that it had several cases of beer.

"That's our man," Billy said, leaving the grill to grab himself a drink. "Now it's a real bonfire."

Charlie did his best to ignore them, turning his back on the newcomers and focusing on the grill. It was actually pretty easy to do considering who was around him. Charade, Jose, Tito, Melinda and Lamar all stuck in a small circle around the grill, just talking and passing time while Charlie and Billy took turns cooking. It was easygoing, and Charlie didn't feel pressured to drink or act like anyone other than himself.

Until he felt a slender hand on his shoulder, and someone pressed in close to him to whisper in his ear.

"Hey, you're one of those Miller heirs, right?"

Charlie couldn't describe the chill that went down his spine. He couldn't turn, he couldn't move, the floor opening up under his feet again.

"Wow, so you're from that mega rich ranching family? That's so cool!"

"You're like, unfairly handsome, did you know that?"

"I bet you get all the girls, a real Casanova type."

"Here, I got you another drink. I call it a Hawaiian Sunrise."

"I heard about your family. I think it's amazing that you've all made a living off the land."

The hand on his shoulder shifted as the woman it belonged to moved to stand in front of him. She was pretty, fresh-faced and tanned, with the smell of hard lemonade on her breath and makeup so immaculate that Clara might even be impressed. But her hair was blond, her eyes were blue, and she looked at him in a way that reminded him of things he never wanted to think of again.

"Hey, you wanna beer? It's good stuff. My dad has his own brewery."

"You're always such a goody two-shoes. Come on, don't you wanna live it up a little?"

"You're way too handsome to be wasting all this. It's like a sin, or something."

"Here, try this. You can't even taste the liquor."

"He's been a big admirer of your family. He said his cousin works as a farmhand up north with the other chunk of your family. Such a small world, isn't it?"

She wasn't being mean. She wasn't even doing anything wrong, and yet Charlie could feel the world spiraling away from him. She was too close. She was too touchy. And she looked far too much—

"Suddenly another hand on his shoulder, but it was grounding, pulling him back to earth. Blinking, he looked beside him to see none other than Daisy.

What was she doing here?

"Hey, sorry to interrupt you, sugar, but I need to talk to my friend here."

The cheerleader frowned but nodded as if she understood. "Okay. I'll look for you later, if you don't mind."

Charlie nodded because that was what humans were supposed to do in such a situation, but he felt like he was detached from his body. But then Daisy went up on her tiptoes and whispered in his ear.

It was the same action as the other girl, and yet it was totally different. But maybe that was because of what she said.

"Please help me," she murmured, sounding absolutely miserable. "I really want a drink right now and I don't know if I can say no."

Oh.

13

———————

Daisy

It was weird that rich, perfect Charles Miller knew about her struggle with sobriety. Point-blank. Daisy was usually pretty protective of that fact, with only her fellow members of AA, Melinda and Billy knowing of her recovery, so Charlie had never been on her short list of people she'd trust with her shame.

But it was also kind of nice.

Charlie wasn't a big drinker. She was pretty sure she'd only seen him with a single beer in his hand once or twice, and two people not drinking while talking at a party was a lot less strange than a single person walking around without any alcohol.

Not to mention that he regularly took her to AA meetings. Normally she'd only go about once every other week and that was enough for her. But since she didn't have Terrance to call for support, and with the stress of having no phone for two weeks, along with her car insurance payment completely depleting her bank account, the stress was mounting much faster than usual. And with stress, came the desire to drink.

It was easy to avoid it during the day while she was busy riding, picking up extra shifts and otherwise being occupied. It wasn't that much harder during nights in the work week either, because she was usually so exhausted that she just collapsed face-first in bed.

But when Monday and Tuesday rolled around... well, those were the real struggle.

She'd been alright the previous week, sticking in her trailer and painting her toenails, then going through the arduous process of putting overnight curlers in her thick, wavy hair. But by the second time the rodeo-weekend rolled around, she was ready to chew her own nails off.

She just wanted a drink. Hadn't she earned one? Would it really be so bad if she indulged just once? She'd been so good for like, two weeks.

But Daisy knew that train of thought and exactly where it led, so she found herself looking for Charlie, weirdly enough. She didn't know why she didn't look for Melinda, or perhaps even Billy, but that wasn't where her mind went. For some reason, it said that Charlie would be the one to talk her down. The one she could trust with the most destructive part of herself.

It wasn't that hard to spot him. She headed toward the bonfire and sure enough, he was standing at the grill with a group of people. Except almost instantly she knew that something was off. His posture was as stiff as a board and his shoulders looked more like earrings than where they were supposed to rest.

And maybe that was because there was a woman with him. She was a pretty young thing, all blond hair and flushed with youth. She had that effortless ease of a college girl, and a very young one at that. Her hand was on Charlie's shoulder and she was leaning in close. She didn't have the same predatory expression that the woman in the bar had, just a genuine grin as she talked animatedly.

But Daisy knew that posture. She didn't know how, but she just *knew*. So she marched forward, all reservations gone, and went right over to him.

Thankfully, the girl left pretty quickly, getting that Daisy was requesting privacy but in a polite way. She actually did seem like a nice person, but that same stressed panic was radiating off Charlie in waves. And before she could think twice about it, she was asking him for help.

And, to her surprise, he agreed.

"What can I do?"

She blinked at him. She'd almost expected him to object or ask if it could wait until later because he was cooking. But no. Just a simple, plain answer.

What did she need?

"A walk would be nice. Let me get some fresh air and get away from... all this." She made a vague gesture to the party around them, and he nodded.

"That would be good, actually. I could use some air myself."

And apparently, it was just that easy.

Daisy was beginning to feel like she owed Charlie an apology.

"Thank you, by the way," he said.

"Hm?" Daisy asked, surprised. Why was he thanking her? She'd interrupted his party experience or something like that.

"You got me away from that situation. I needed it."

It all clicked into place, and she remembered how he'd been standing, how she'd gone up to him on instinct. How had that slipped her mind so quickly? "You okay, by the way? You seemed pretty tense."

"It's getting better now. I just needed space."

"I understand that. It's easy to feel crowded real fast at a good bonfire."

They walked along quietly, heading to the edge of the parking lot, which was really just a flattened field, but it served its purpose well enough. It was nice, just listening to the sound of the nighttime creatures that dominated the summer. The urge to drink began to fade, sinking down into a low murmur in the back of her mind.

But then Charlie was speaking again. "How did you know?"

"Know what?" Geez, she sounded like such a dork. Maybe composing a complete sentence would be a good move.

"You helped me at the bar. You helped me at this party. I know it's not usual for someone to freeze up in front of a beautiful woman, so it's not like this is something that you've had tons of experience with. It's weird."

Oh wow, there was a whole lot of baggage there. Daisy could hear it, even with him facing away from her, layered throughout his words.

"Everyone's weird in their own way. And, if I'm being honest, I didn't ride in to save the day or anything like that. I was panicking and I needed help, so I just made a beeline to you. I noticed you were stressed from that girl, but I don't want to pretend like I'm some sort of martyr."

He was quiet again for a while. "You came straight to me for help?"

"Yeah. Now who do you think is the weird one?"

He chuckled ever so slightly, and it was a good sound, a homey sort of warm sound that she wished she heard more often. "Alright, maybe neither of us are very qualified on what's weird or not."

"I think that's a fair statement."

They shared a small laugh together, and it was nice. Just... *nice.* Nothing big or dramatic, just a sweet sort of comfort at the end of a really stressful day.

"You're something else, aren't you?" he asked finally.

"I might have been told that before." Daisy shrugged. "But when it comes to your whole lady situation, I can tell you're uncomfortable. It's basically like a blaring sign over your head, and it's just... well, to me it seems wrong to stand there and not do anything when it's so easy to just say something."

He sank into silence again, their footsteps a counter rhythm to the buzzing of insects and faint sounds of traffic from far away. For a moment, Daisy was worried that he might think she was overbearing or nosey, but instead he sighed.

"I wish more people had instincts like yours."

Oh.

Well, that was nice.

She didn't know what to say to that, so they slipped into silence again. But it wasn't uncomfortable. There was a peacefulness to it, and it cloaked Daisy like a blanket that she didn't even know she'd been missing.

They just walked. They walked and they breathed in the fresh air, and Daisy felt her emotions slowly begin to settle. She could have thanked Charlie for his time, dismissed herself, and headed back to her trailer, and yet she kept walking. Even when they completed their entire circuit of the parking lot and turned to head toward the animal pens.

"I think most of them are going to be asleep," she said finally.

"I agree. They're pretty good at following their routines. But sometimes I feel better when I'm around animals."

"You have those on the ranch, I'm guessing?"

"We're not a big ranch like my cousins', but we have goats, a few horses, and a whole lot of chickens. Clara *loves* chickens."

"That sounds like an eccentric interest."

"Maybe, but I think it's from my aunt down in Texas. Clara stayed down there for a couple weeks one summer and she fell in love with Auntie's coop."

He smiled at her, a soft and tender expression that made Daisy's breath catch. She was rooted to the spot, unsure what to say, but then an irritated huff sounded beside them.

Daisy jumped, recoiling until she realized that it was one of the stallions reprimanding them for being too loud.

"Geez, Kamehameha, you startled me," she chided, trying not to laugh hysterically. But *goodness,* the look on the horse's face was something else.

"Maybe we should head back. I wouldn't want to disturb his beauty sleep any more than we already have."

"Aww, I want to stick with the animals a while longer. I really don't get to spend enough time with them."

"I know what you mean. I spent about three hours in the goat pen back home last week."

"I wish that I could do that. Just pet all of those goat babies and spoil all of Clara's chickens until they like me more than her."

He snorted, yet it wasn't an unattractive sound. Weird.

"You'd be hard-pressed to do that. Clara is uncannily good with animals."

"I'm up to the challenge."

"Alright then. Come over."

Daisy froze halfway to walking over to Kamehameha. "What did you say?"

"If you want to try to knock Clara off the chicken throne, you're more than welcome to try. I'll drive you there this Monday and Tuesday."

Was a millionaire really inviting her into his home like it was just that easy?

Apparently so.

"I think I'd like that."

"Alright then. You'll need to wake up early, though. We'll leave by seven."

And that was that.

14

Daisy

*D*aisy decided that if heaven was real, it was a ranch.

She'd been bleary-eyed and half-asleep when she stumbled into Charlie's truck. But after being able to nap on the drive to his place, she felt much more refreshed when she arrived at the most non-mansion-looking mansion she'd ever seen.

It was made of wood, glass and stone, arranged in a natural, cottage core sort of vibe. It reminded Daisy of *Little House on the Prairie* or *Secret Garden* except about twenty times bigger.

Two gardens took over the yard out front. One a large, verdant one that she guessed was their edible garden, and then a truly impressive flower one in the front. Daisy wasn't the best gardener, but she recognized scarlet, cosmos, roses, sunflowers and carnations. There seemed to be just about every color possible and some that were even multiple colors. It was like walking into a fairy world.

And it just kept getting better.

Charlie gave her a tour of the inside of the cabin-mansion, and the inside was just as perfect as the out. Daisy had almost expected tacky huntsman chic or that overly minimalistic modern style that was all the rage among rich people, but instead it was the perfect mix of natural, practical and clean lines.

Sure, most everything was either wood or stone, but it worked well together. Especially since plants were all over the place. Plenty of family photos, trophies or art, added splashes of color and life to so many places.

It probably wasn't supposed to be a mind-blowing tour, he was just showing her where the kitchen was if she got thirsty and the bathroom was if she needed to use it, but Daisy was impressed nonetheless.

And that wasn't even counting the Millers she kept encountering at different points. Each of them seemed genuinely happy to see her, and the one in the wheelchair ribbed Charlie so thoroughly that Daisy's cheeks were hurting by the time the one that had to be Clara came out of the kitchen and told her to play nice. In just twenty minutes, it was easy for Daisy to see that the family really, truly loved each other.

And she was jealous of that in the best way.

Her relationship with her mother was nonexistent, and honestly, Daisy didn't miss it. They had been toxic together, with her mother being emotionally abusive and full of hate and Daisy falling into all the normal troubles that came along with being an alcoholic by the ripe old age of eighteen. Her father? He'd never been in the picture. She didn't even know his name. And with no siblings, no aunts, no uncles, it'd been just her for almost a full decade.

And she'd always told herself she liked it that way.

But seeing how the Millers interacted, she couldn't help but wonder how much she'd missed.

Oh well, it wasn't like she could go back in time and get her mother the therapy she needed, so what was done was done.

Besides, Daisy didn't get a chance to linger over that thought long because then they were going outside and meeting all the animals.

Funny, for working at a rodeo, Daisy had no idea that chickens came in so many varieties. There were pretty, fluffy ones that looked like they were wearing disco bellbottoms. Tiny ones that looked like they had fur more than feathers. And speckled ones. Ones with giant tails that were almost like horse manes. Red ones, black ones, white ones, dappled ones, the list went on and on.

And pretty much every chicken in Clara's flock loved humans.

Daisy found herself surrounded almost immediately, and it was the absolute best. But somehow, best got even better when Charlie gave her a feed bucket and then she really was the star of the pen.

She'd thought it couldn't get any better than that, but then he'd taken her to the goat pen and that was truly *magical.*

Apparently, they'd had an impressive amount of kidding in the early spring, and due to some trauma with one of the mothers, Clara had had to bottle feed the two doelings and buckling. They called them 'bottle babies.' The bottle feeding resulted in some *incredibly* people-oriented kids who practically ran to the gate, their tails wagging almost too fast to see.

Goats could wag their tails. Who knew? Certainly not her.

Despite her situation as a show rider, Daisy only ever dealt with horses and bulls. Not exactly an extensive agricultural background.

So, it was great. Better than great. Amazing stacked on top of wonderful stuffed inside a whole roll of fun. She was so caught up in it, all of it, that she definitely had to do a double-take when Charlie asked her if she was ready for lunch.

"But we just got here."

"Daisy, it's after one. We've been here since eight AM."

Daisy just stared at him for several moments before looking for the position of the sun.

"It *is* past noon."

"Hah, don't worry. You're not the only one that's happened to. Come on. I know Clara has probably gone overboard with whatever she made for lunch."

"Wait, your sister cooks a custom lunch for y'all too?"

"It depends on how she's feeling. Sometimes Papa does, and sometimes it's just leftovers. But you better believe whenever we have a guest that she makes sure there's a full spread available."

Maybe Daisy should have been more incredulous, but suddenly Charlie's bizarre interest in taking care of her made a lot of sense.

Huh.

"We better head inside then. If your sister's lunch is anything like her hangover cure, I'm sure it's going to be great."

"Oh, you have no idea."

It turned out that he was absolutely right.

Somehow, in the five or so hours since she'd been gone, Clara had made roast beef sandwiches on buttery rolls that were still warm to the touch, deviled eggs, cucumber sandwiches, tea, fried chicken and coleslaw. There was also a pitcher of reddish-looking tea on the table as well as a pot of coffee.

"There you are," the infamous Clara said, clapping her hands once she saw them. "I was just about to send for you."

Daisy felt herself blush slightly. She liked to think she was a person who was difficult to ruffle, but something about the middle Miller sister made her flustered. She was a tall bird, that was for sure. Easily over five foot ten, plus she was wearing cute wedge sandals with pink flowers on the front.

It wasn't just that she was tall either. She was dressed in a retro sort of getup and had her hair done up in impeccable curls. She was basically the perfect image of a 1950s housewife, except with biceps that looked like she could have a serious career in arm wrestling.

Basically, she was impeccably put together and sweet as pie, and that made Daisy feel... lacking.

"Don't worry, Clara. I wouldn't let anybody miss out on your cooking."

"Good. I've trained you well."

He snorted, pulling out a chair for Daisy like it wasn't anything. And who knew, maybe for him, it wasn't a big deal, but Daisy felt herself flush again. She wasn't the type of girl that guys pulled out chairs for, but Charlie did it like it was a matter of course.

She was saved from ruminating over that too long, however, because the eldest sister was striding in again. Or at least she tried to, until Clara suddenly whirled with a pointed finger.

"Charity Miller, if you are about to tromp on my clean kitchen floor without taking off those oily boots, you better think twice on it."

The woman stopped, grinning widely as she took off one

boot and then the other. "I don't know how you're able to tell that without even looking at me."

"God has blessed me with a very acute ability to sense a mess approaching," Clara retorted primly.

"Your shop boots squeak."

That was Cass, coming in through the front door, a beautiful cane in one of her hands and a tall, handsome man beside her.

A *really* handsome man.

Daisy didn't think she'd ever seen a black cowboy outside of the rodeo she worked for, but the dark-skinned man was absolutely that. He was wearing dark, rough and tumble jeans, a purple button-up and thick gloves on his hands. He had on a fancy cowboy hat, which Daisy knew had to have been a pretty penny. Not like any of the cheap, internet ones that she'd bedazzled.

"Oh look, everyone is here," Clara said, clapping her hands.

"Where are Papa and Cici?" Charlie asked.

Daisy began to have trouble remembering who was who. Cici was... the youngest? Maybe? She felt like she had heard that before.

"They're off to a museum that just opened in the city," Charity said, sitting down at the table with a pair of house slippers on to replace her boots. Daisy had no idea where she'd gotten those house slippers, but they were on her feet nonetheless.

"I'm hoping to go there next month," Cass said, dropping down into her own chair and the quiet man sat next to her. He looked once to Daisy and gave a slight nod, then that was that. A man of few words, apparently.

That was fine. Daisy was never one of those people who insisted that other people needed to talk as much as she did.

Besides, considering that she was surrounded by several Miller characters, she wasn't exactly feeling verbose herself.

Besides, who needed to talk when there was delicious food to stuff down her face?

And *boy*, was the food *good*.

Clara's hangover cure hadn't been a fluke. Everything was tasty, flavorful and utterly delicious. The chicken was crispy and had a dash of spice to it. The cucumber sandwiches were dainty and crisp, while the roast beef sandwiches tasted like... Daisy didn't know the exact way to describe it, but the closest adjective that came to mind was that it tasted how home should feel.

Weird.

She would have to investigate by eating another sandwich. It was a real trial, of course.

"I hope this isn't rude, but I think I recognize you from the barrel shows," Clara said while Daisy's mouth was full of her mystifyingly delicious sandwich. "You're Scarlet, aren't you?"

Geez, Clara saw her at shows? The woman had a pleasant smile on her face, but one could never tell what some people thought of rodeo performers. There were plenty of people who were fans and would launch into a flurry of curious questions, but plenty of people had negative opinions. Especially when it came to a young, unmarried woman spending so much of her time with all of those 'rough types.'

Daisy swallowed hard. "That's me."

"I thought so. You're always so fun to watch, but I'm sure you know that."

"Ah, I appreciate that."

"Of course." She lowered her head like she was sharing something conspiratorial. "You do have some of the most fun costumes of any of the riders."

"Here we go," Charity said with a chuckle.

"Wait, where are we going?" Daisy interjected, feeling like she was missing something everyone else was in on.

"Clara is the result of when a costume lover meets a fashion lover and you throw a vintage glam obsession in," Cass said, grinning from across the table. "And she's trying to think of a subtle way to rope you into letting her dress you up."

"What?"

"Now Cass, why do you have to do that to me?" Clara grumped, her chin in her hand. She pouted at her sister before her gaze returned to Daisy. It was almost cute how she looked both bashful and hopeful at the same time. "But if you ever were willing, I have a couple of designs I've been working on."

Aww, it was sweet, undeniably so. Although Daisy knew she'd never be able to afford the proper materials or a living wage for the heiress, she was touched nonetheless. "I'd have to look at my budget, but maybe in—"

"You wouldn't have to pay for it," Clara objected before she could finish, eyes wide. "This is just something I do for fun. You would be making a dream of mine come true, getting to watch a professional wear *my* design in front of a cheering crowd. I should probably pay *you*."

...what even were the Millers? Daisy felt like she needed to be pinched, just to be sure the moment was real.

"You wouldn't need to pay me at all. But if you really want to, I'd be more than happy to model anything you made."

The woman clapped her hands again and Daisy was beginning to get the idea that was one of her mannerisms. It was easy to see why Rick had been pining over the woman for so long, and equally easy to see why he'd always been too intimidated to approach her. Daisy felt that being in her presence was like looking exactly at the sun.

"If you let me take your measurements before you leave, I could probably have something whipped up for you in a week or two. That will be in time for the rest of the season, right? I know you've only got two months left."

"Two and a half months, actually. And then we move south to hook up with the Kapner rodeo for a joint gig."

"So you'll have plenty of time to use it. Amazing! Thank you so much."

She smiled so brightly that Daisy felt like she needed shades. But then someone was patting her hand and she looked over to see it was Cass, who was sending her a wry grin.

"Don't worry. You get used to it after a while. I swear, we're mostly normal people."

"If you squint," Charity added from the head of the table.

"And do a handstand," Charlie added, grinning impishly.

They all laughed, and Daisy joined in, even if she wasn't quite sure she got the whole joke. But it was easy to laugh with the Millers, especially with their banter flowing like water. They were all so comfortable with each other that it felt easy to slip into the comfortableness with them.

Daisy had never really had a family, only in the vaguest definition of the word, but as she sat there surrounded by the tall, striking people, she couldn't help but feel that *this* was exactly what family was supposed to be.

And it was nice.

Real nice.

'Lunch' ended up lasting several hours, only ending when Clara dismissed herself to go to her fiancé's house with dinner that had apparently been cooking while they were all talking. Daisy thought that Clara could probably have her own cooking show, her food was that good, but she would need to investigate further before deciding.

And by investigate, she meant eat more sinfully delicious meals. Yum.

At that point Daisy was sure Charlie would tell her it was time to go, but then Charity leaned over with a pleasant expression on her face.

"You look capable. Want to see my workshop?"

Tools weren't entirely Daisy's thing, but she liked understanding how things were put together, so she nodded immediately.

"Sounds like a good time to me."

And it was a good time. There was plenty of stuff that Daisy didn't quite understand, but seeing all the farm equipment that Charity maintained or repaired and how Cassidy apparently kept it all organized was utterly fascinating. Daisy had known that there was a whole lot that went into farming, but she felt like someone was pulling back the curtain so she could see backstage.

And it was so cool.

She ended up spending several hours there, Charlie in the background adding to the conversation, until another younger woman came bounding up, throwing herself at Charlie first, then Charity before carefully hugging Cass last. She shared similar features to all three of the siblings and Daisy guessed that this was the missing Cici.

"Hey, Cici," Charity said, confirming Daisy's perspective. "How was the museum?"

"It was so great," the college girl answered, her voice jam-packed full of excitement. "The exhibits were really interesting and there wasn't that much of a crowd. Papa was—Oh! Who's this?"

Suddenly the girl's intense gaze was on Daisy and *wow*, Daisy missed when she used to have that much energy.

"Hi, my name is Daisy. I work with your brother Charlie at the rodeo."

"What, really? Wait, that's how I know you. You're that cool rider who does the mid-show, right? I totally love your outfits!"

"You come to the rodeo? I don't think I've ever seen you there."

"I only go once or twice a year maybe, but I've been having my sisters stream when you and that other cool riding lady go. What's her name? She's super pale, has jet black hair?"

"That's Annie Winrock."

"I'm so sad she broke her leg this year. That's such a bummer for everyone."

"It's rough, but she'll be back next year."

The girl nodded before jumping from foot to foot. "Oh! Oh! Has anyone shown you the garden yet?"

Charlie chuckled behind her. "No, we saved that for you, shortstack."

"Hey, just because you're all giants doesn't mean I'm short. I'll have you know, I'm two inches above average for women in America." Cici heaved a long-suffering sigh and sent Daisy a martyred look. "Do you see what I have to deal with?"

"I do. It must be tough being the youngest."

"Hah, that's an understatement! But anyway, come with me. Let me show you all the things we grow."

And that was how she found herself being hauled all the way to the front of the yard by Cici and given a thorough tour of what seemed like millions of heirlooms, hybrids and whatever else they were growing. It probably should have been boring, but Cici's enthusiasm was so infectious that Daisy thoroughly enjoyed herself. It also helped that Cici kept picking things and putting them in a basket for her. Daisy wasn't going to have to worry about an empty mini-fridge for at least a week, and she couldn't remember the last time she could afford so much fresh produce.

Daisy had no idea how long they were out until it became hard to see. Looking up, she realized the sun was setting.

"Wait, how late is it?"

"Huh? Oh goodness, it's almost nine o'clock."

"I hope you don't mind I didn't interrupt," Charlie said from where he was weeding one of the beds. Daisy had almost forgotten that he was there. Whoops. "You two just seemed like you were having too much fun."

"That's because we were," Cici said, just as energetic as she had been when she first bounced into Charity's mechanic shop. "Are you hungry?"

Daisy was going to say that no, she'd just eaten lunch, but she realized that was actually all the way back at one o'clock and she hadn't eaten in hours. "I could eat something."

"Come on. I bet Papa has cooked something delicious."

The young woman grabbed her hand and hauled Daisy back inside, where sure enough, there was indeed a yummy dinner laid out. It wasn't as elaborate as Clara's lunch, but it was still a delicious dish of beef and noodles that Daisy had never had before.

The second meal was quieter than the first, with both Charity and Clara missing, but still enjoyable. Daisy was still nervous around the Miller patriarch, but he had such a calming presence that her nerves never got too frayed.

Once more she was struck by that feeling of belonging. Which was completely ridiculous, considering that she hadn't even spent a full day with the family and they were literal millionaires. She had more in common with an ant than the Millers, and yet...

"Geez, this meal is really hitting me hard," Charlie said, hiding a pretty egregious yawn behind his hand. "We better hurry back to the rodeo. I don't like driving sleepy."

It was crazy, but Daisy realized she didn't want to go. The ranch was like an escape from all of her stresses. No bills. No responsibilities. She didn't even have a craving for a cold beer. She just wanted to stay with the affectionate goats and the diva chickens and forget all the things that were pulling her down.

But all good things must come to an end, she supposed. She'd enjoyed her day of charity, but it was important not to get greedy. After all—

"Son, you're already looking pretty tired." Suddenly Papa Miller's eyes were on her. "I don't mean to be an imposition on you, miss, but we have plenty of guest rooms. If you don't mind staying the night, I'm sure Clara would love to send you off with a delicious breakfast and I'd be much obliged."

...could he read her mind, or had she been telegraphing her disappointment that broadly? Either way, she knew she was too eager when she responded. Oh well.

"I don't mind at all. I don't have anything pressing at home and I'm pretty bushed too."

That wasn't a lie. Daisy couldn't remember when she'd had

such a full day that wasn't work-related. And although she'd missed out on the chance to pick up another overtime shift, she was more than happy to milk as much happiness out of her version of the weekend as she could.

"Well, it's settled then. Cici, would you—"

"I'd love to."

And that was that.

They finished up the meal and then Daisy was being ushered upstairs by the youngest Miller for another tour of the upper floor. The staircase was fairly impressive, but apparently the Millers had a whole *elevator* in their house. At first Daisy was completely baffled, but then she remembered the second oldest sister had mobility issues and was healing from some sort of accident.

It was amazing what money could do.

Eventually Daisy found herself in a fairly spacious room with a luxurious bed and then an *attached* bathroom. And it wasn't an empty shell of a room either. There were fluffy towels, a bathrobe, multiple bath products and just about anything else Daisy could ever want.

Crazy.

"Alright, you have a good night now. I hope I see you in the morning, but I'm not as early a riser as my siblings."

"You have a good night too, Cici."

She bounced out, leaving Daisy standing alone in the middle of a guest room in a house full of millionaires. Half wondering if she was dreaming, the cowgirl went about taking the most luxurious bath she could before tucking herself into bed.

But as she settled onto the cloudy mattress with its amazing blankets, she couldn't help but wonder if her life would have been different if she'd been raised like the Millers had. Would she have been an alcoholic? Would she have gone to college?

It was hard to say.

But wondering 'what if' was usually a waste of energy, and Daisy was tapped out. So she closed her eyes and allowed herself to drift off.

15

Daisy

Daisy woke up half expecting to be in her ratty trailer with her entire day at the Miller Ranch being a fever dream that couldn't possibly be true. But then she realized her back felt supported just right and she wasn't freezing cold or burning hot. Her belly wasn't aching with hunger and her head wasn't pounding, her brain begging to be fed.

Slowly, she opened her eyes, and sure enough she was in the same luxurious room that she'd fallen asleep in. And she was not complaining one bit.

Practically bouncing out of bed, Daisy grabbed her phone from where it was charging on the vanity and saw that she'd woken up forty minutes before her alarm. She couldn't remember the last time she had done that. Usually, she was so exhausted and worn out that she would hit snooze about five times and still be exhausted when she stumbled out of her trailer.

Huh, it was amazing what a supportive bed set up, a hot bath, and a couple of meals could do for her. She had no idea how she was going to go back to her thin roll of foam on the floor, but that was for Daisy to deal with later.

Not wanting to miss any time that she could squeeze out of her ranch experience, Daisy bounded down the stairs. She knew that most people would assume she was a country girl considering her line of work, but she'd lived in the city her entire life before she was homeless—converted to living in her car. It had been her boyfriend when she was sixteen who worked part-time as a stable hand. A lot of times she would go to his shift and sit around just to have something to do other than have her mother scream at her. She didn't know if she looked particularly dejected or if the owner of the stables thought she was pretty, because he'd offered to teach her how to ride a horse, and from there... well, things were history.

But she'd always been curious about farm life, especially with all the stories she'd heard from other workers and rodeo attendees. It seemed antiquated in some ways, but so peaceful in others. Now that she'd actually spent time on the ranch, she could see why so many people loved it so much. *She* loved it so much. Maybe, if she was real nice to Charlie, he would let her come over again.

Wouldn't that be nice.

"Whoa, I didn't expect to see you up so early."

And speaking of the handsome cowboy himself. Daisy liked to think that she was used to the man's sort of classic attractiveness, but she was never prepared for seeing him standing in his kitchen in his gray pajamas, his head still mussed from sleep. His eyes were just bleary enough to be adorable, and there was that morning flush to his cheeks that made the strong bone structure of the Miller family stand out that much stronger.

Gosh, he was handsome.

"Hi," Daisy croaked. "I slept really well."

"I'll say. Clara's out in the back tending to the chickens if you're still serious about trying to usurp her throne."

Daisy couldn't help but laugh at that. "After meeting her, I now realize my quest was futile. But I wouldn't mind going out to help her anyway if you think she'd welcome me."

"I'm sure she'd love to have you out there. If only because you're a new person that she can tell all her favorite chicken stories to."

Daisy couldn't think of a better way to spend her morning.

Charlie led her out to the impressive coop in the back. The chickens weren't exactly inside, however. Most of them gathered around Clara who looked like she was handing out treats. Daisy wasn't sure what constituted treats to chickens, but there were some things that translated on any animal, and the excitement over a special food was pretty universal.

"Oh, hey there. Cici told me you'd spent the night. Any requests for breakfast?"

"Honestly, I'm fine with whatever you serve. I'm pretty easy to please."

"I'll just do the usual then."

"Her food is less greasy than Gert's," Charlie whispered, leaning down so only she would hear his words.

Instantly, goosebumps broke out along her arms. Oh... that was certainly something.

Charlie continued. "But it's still just as delicious. Maybe more delicious. It's hard to say. Gert is pretty incredible."

Daisy swallowed hard, her tongue apparently having forgotten how to lay right in her mouth. "Uh-huh."

In another moment of serendipity, a chicken walked up to her and warbled insistently until Daisy picked it up, giving her something else to focus on instead of the rushing feeling shooting through her. Sure, it had been a while since she'd had any fun dates, but that was by choice. She was so busy and stressed over finances that something as frivolous as a date seemed more exhausting than enjoyable.

But suddenly she was acutely aware of just how close Charlie was to her and just how good-looking he was.

No, good-looking wasn't the right word. More like drop-dead gorgeous and completely unfair.

"I'm going to go get dressed then wash off some of the equipment while we're here. Are you going to be okay with all these hens?" he asked.

"I dunno. They are direct descendants of dinosaurs, you know."

Charlie grinned, shaking his head at her, and that made her stomach flip like it was in the Olympics. Weird. "Well, if they start chasing you through the tall grass, remember to zigzag."

"Would that actually help?"

"I don't know. Remind me to ask the next dinosaur expert I happen to run into."

"I'll make sure to do that."

Chuckling, he gave that little salute he liked to do and headed off, leaving her with the chickens. After a while, Clara asked if she'd like to help her check the nesting boxes for eggs, and Daisy didn't think she'd ever agreed to a chore so fast in her life.

From there they went inside, and Clara didn't mind Daisy helping along with breakfast too. And by help, that meant it was mostly clearing dishes and handing Clara the cooking diva things.

But still, it was so... *nice.* Daisy knew that she should stop using that word, but it just fit so right. It was easy to imagine how much better her life would have been if she'd been surrounded by people like the Millers instead of the cards she'd actually been handed.

And geez, to think she'd thought Charlie was arrogant. The truth was, he was the furthest thing from it.

Daisy felt bad about how she'd misinterpreted him. It was clear that Charlie had a thing about being touched, and he was a real homebody. Given what his home was like, she couldn't actually blame him. But she'd totally taken his flinching and tension as judgment, as elitism and disdain, when really it was just his discomfort.

And the truth was she'd been jealous about his money. She knew that. It didn't seem fair that some people never had to struggle in their life while she was busy deciding if she could even eat for the day. But Charlie couldn't help that he was born to a wealthy family any more than she could help that she was born to a mother that never wanted her. It was clear that his family wasn't out of touch or spoiled and shared their wealth with pretty much everyone around them.

Hindsight was funny like that, she supposed. It certainly made it a lot easier to see how her own bitterness had tinted her view of things.

How much time had she wasted by setting things off on the wrong foot? Then again, it was him who'd come up to her in the middle of her telling a story to her friends to tell her to tone the swearing down. Not really a great way to start a friendship.

Oh well. Everyone had bad days, and she was glad they were past that now.

Breakfast turned out just as enjoyable and delicious as the other meals, and when it was over, Clara asked her if she wanted to go out and milk the goats. Apparently, she normally would do it earlier, but since Charlie had said how much she'd enjoyed playing with them the day before, she'd waited so Daisy could join her.

Daisy was pretty sure that Clara was a saint.

It was interesting learning how the woman got her goats into the milking stands and her process of taking care of the flock. Her goats were so incredibly well-behaved, but they still had plenty of personality. Especially Bilbo, Arwen and Eowyn. Daisy couldn't be sure, but she had a feeling the goats had actively tried to prank her several times, and she'd only avoided it because of Clara's warning.

Daisy wished that she could stay there forever. But eventually the goats were all handled, there was a quick trip to drop off garden scraps to the pigs for a treat, and then it was time to go. She wished she could stay, she really did, but they did need to get back to the rodeo and prep for work starting the next day.

"You ready?" Charlie asked her.

No, she wasn't, but she knew it was time. She still needed to haul her clothes and bedding to the laundromat and get all the produce she'd been given into her mini-fridge. Not to mention she needed to check in with Melinda and Billy. Thankfully, she'd been able to connect to the Miller's WiFi so she was able to message them that way, but she was sure they were expecting her back.

Once more, the ride was fairly quiet on their return, the radio still playing quietly. Daisy wasn't sure what was on Charlie's mind, but hers was going over everything that had happened, playing each moment in detail so she would never forget it. The next time she had an intense craving to break her vow of sobriety, she would think of the peace and happiness that she'd experienced on the Miller Ranch and remind herself that that kind of joy couldn't be found in a bottle.

And who knew, maybe it would actually work.

For the first time in a long, long while, Daisy actually had hope for the future. That maybe not everything had to be a struggle. That tomorrow could be more than a fight to survive and there could be something bright in her future. And that was more valuable than anything else she could have asked for.

She owed Charlie so much, and she didn't think he had a clue.

But that was okay, because he had a staunch ally in her now. She was going to be the best, best, bestest friend he could ask for and give him whatever support he needed. If she had to chase off eager ladies with baseball bats, she would.

And maybe, if she was by his side long enough, he would be comfortable enough to have her at his side.

Whoa. Let's not get ahead of ourselves.

They had one good weekend together. That's it. It wasn't like they were star-crossed lovers or main characters in a romantic comedy. They were just two coworkers, and Charlie was just exceptionally nice with a few social hang-ups. That's it.

But still... it was easy to let her mind wander. Suddenly the 'what if' didn't seem so taboo.

If Charlie noticed that she was entirely in her head, he didn't say so. But when they arrived at the rodeo, he parked as close as he could get to her trailer then walked her all the way to her door.

She didn't know what came over her; maybe it was the full belly, or maybe it was that she was still floating on the wonderful haze of the ranch. But right before she was supposed to go into her door, she suddenly turned to Charlie.

"Hey, would you want to go on a date sometime?"

Oh no.

Oh *no.*

Her free hand instantly covered her mouth as dread swamped her. They'd just repaired their contentious relationship and she'd gone and ruined it. She *knew* Charlie had a hang-up with women coming onto him, and yet she'd just done the same thing. She'd violated his trust after everything he'd done for her. How ungrateful could she get?

But the expression on his face wasn't angry, or horrified, or gray and completely frozen like it had been at the bar. Instead a slow, warm smile spread across his handsome features.

"Yeah, I think that'd be great."

...oh.

16

———————

Charlie

Charlie licked his lips, stomach flipping as he drove along. He was going on a date. A real, honest-to-goodness date with a beautiful woman.

He was pretty sure he was crazy.

He hadn't been on a date since he was a freshman in college. He had assumed he'd never go on one again. And yet, here he was, driving into the city with Daisy talking animatedly beside him, ready to go see a movie and have dinner.

He was nervous, that was for certain, and part of his mind was running a constant diatribe of how ridiculous he was to even try. How was he supposed to have a successful date when sometimes even being touched by a woman made him want to heave? How could he give her a goodnight kiss when he hadn't touched a woman since, well, college?

But then he'd look at Daisy, at her wide grin and her laughter-pinkened cheeks, and that negative voice inside his head would get quieter and quieter.

He had never anticipated anything happening between the two of them. But when she'd saved him for the second time and they'd walked around the entire parking lot, he felt a trust toward her that he hadn't felt towards a stranger in a long time. That skin-crawling feeling was gone. He didn't have to be on high alert. He could just be himself.

And he liked himself around Daisy.

So, when she'd wistfully murmured about wanting to see the animals on his farm, how could he not jump at the chance to give her that? Besides that night that she asked him to help her not drink, he didn't think he'd ever heard Daisy ask for something, and his mouth had gone off without his brain again. He'd expected her to refuse, of course, but then she'd surprised him by saying yes.

And then he'd thought that taking her to the ranch would either be awkward at best or a disaster at worst, but it was nothing like that. In fact, almost from the moment that they were home, she fit right in like she belonged. Like she was *meant* to be there.

Or maybe Charlie was just crazy.

But crazy or not, he hadn't wanted her to leave. Although he loved the rodeo, he didn't want to leave the safe bubble of the ranch. His home was his safe haven, his refuge, and finding out that Daisy fit in there like a missing puzzle piece made it hard to resist the feeling like he had everything that he could possibly need.

He knew it couldn't last, however, so he'd forced himself to take her home. They'd been quiet on the ride back, Charlie thinking too hard to really give any brainpower toward conversation, but he'd never expected for Daisy to turn to him and ask him out.

He should have said no. He knew his hang-ups and that he couldn't be a good date, or maybe even a boyfriend to her, but he didn't. He selfishly said yes.

And he couldn't bring himself to be mad about it.

On the way to the theater, Daisy was almost bouncing in the seat next to him. "I can't tell you the last time I actually saw a movie in the theater. This is gonna be great!"

Charlie nodded, concentrating as he left the highway. He'd suggested a movie because it meant he wouldn't have to be nervous about keeping up conversation, and he could ease into the whole dating thing after over seven years of avoiding it entirely. It had been an added bonus that Daisy was absolutely thrilled at the suggestion.

How had he ever thought that she was prickly? She was determined, sure, and she was brusque, but she never went out of her way to be hurtful. Once Charlie had gotten to know her— be rescued by her—he'd only ever seen her help people.

And desperately help herself.

Perhaps that was the part of her that enchanted him the most. Charlie had experienced plenty of trauma in his life. From the loss of his mother all the way to Cass's horrendous accident and ensuing healing. But he'd always had his family to rely on. Whenever he felt weak, he could go to Papa and be reaffirmed. When he was frustrated, he could cook with Clara in the kitchen or fix machinery with Charity. When he felt useless, he could go build something that would help his family. And that wasn't even considering the animals themselves. While he was no Clara, he still got a lot of joy and support from the various creatures that called the ranch home.

Daisy didn't have any of that.

As far as he could tell, she had her friends at the rodeo and that was it.

And that made him mad.

Wait, no, maybe mad wasn't the right term. But it made him want to protect her, to give her a shelter like he had. Everyone deserved that, right?

Right?

"Oh shoot. I forgot to bring my snack bag."

"Your what?"

"My snack bag. I didn't have a chance to get much, but I had a few goodies stashed away. Also, I was able to make some poor man's salsa with all those veggies Cici gave me."

It was like she was talking another language. "Do you have diet restrictions or something?"

"No, why do you ask?"

Charlie pulled into the parking lot of the IMAX and sent her a quizzical look. "If you don't need special food, why do you need to bring extra snacks? They have to have something you like in there, don't they?"

She stared at him for a long moment before shaking her head. "Sorry, I'm not judging you. I'm just reeling at some different life experiences. Give me a sec." She shook her head once more, huffed a tiny laugh, then continued. "I bring a snack bag because I love munching during a good movie, but the snacks they have here are so insanely expensive that I could never afford them."

"Oh."

Charlie had never thought about it. In fact, he never even

looked at how much things cost. He would just hand over his card and that was that. He hadn't realized that some people would have to sneak stuff in just to enjoy something as simple as a snack.

"You don't have to worry about that tonight," was all he could say, and he hoped that didn't sound patronizing. But he did resolve to pay attention to the prices.

"You don't have to. I'll be fine. I actually ate lunch today so I'm not starving."

"What do you mean, you actually ate lunch?"

But she just waved his concern off like it wasn't a big deal. But if there was one thing that *was* a big deal to the Millers, it was that everyone around them had full stomachs. What was the point of having money if you knew people who were hungry?

"You know how busy it gets at the rodeo. Who has time to stop and eat in the middle of the day? I just aim for breakfast and dinner. Unless, of course, there's free food. Rule number one of life, you never pass up free food."

There was so much story behind her casual words that Charlie wanted to hug her and tell her that she shouldn't have to live like that. That he wanted to make sure she always had enough to eat and never had to worry. It made him wonder about just the kind of life she was living. He'd seen her small, meager space. He'd seen how what little she owned was falling apart, and that felt so *wrong* to him. Someone who worked as hard as Daisy should have so *much*, but as far as he could tell, she had so *little.*

But he didn't say any of that, mostly because the intensity of his own feelings surprised even him. Instead, he went for humor. Humor was always safe, and at the moment, he felt like he could use a little safety.

"Funny. I would have thought the first rule of life was making sure you had oxygen."

"I mean sure, if you want to be *technical*." She rolled her eyes in that good-natured way people always did after a bad joke, then went to slip out of the Jeep.

Well, that wouldn't do.

It certainly took some pep in his step, but Charlie managed to get out and go around to her side so he could open her door and hold his hand out for her.

"Oh…" she murmured, eyes going wide as her seatbelt made a comically loud sound compared to the sudden quiet between them.

Whoops. Had Charlie just gone and made things awkward?

"Uh, thank you." There was another moment's hesitance where she looked at his hand. "Are you sure?"

Charlie wasn't quite sure what she meant at first, but then he remembered that she'd seen him freeze up at unwanted touch twice. And although he more than wanted to have her hands in his, it struck him as particularly sweet that she would even care to ask.

"Yes, I'm sure."

Her cheeks were ever so slightly pink as she ducked her head, and then her hand slid into his.

It was rough, calloused and ever so slightly dry, just like one would expect a rodeo worker's hand would be. Especially one who spent so much time picking up extra jobs, many of which involved using strong cleaners to keep the rodeo in good condition.

But it still felt *right* there, sending a different sort of sensation along Charlie's skin. And as he helped her to the ground, it brought them close to each other, and he didn't feel that usual pool of dread in his stomach. No, instead he found himself studying her face. Noting every single freckle, every variation in her skin. He wanted to remember how her eyes reflected the streetlight above them to make it look like something far more magical, how her thick hair was pulled back into a high ponytail that made her heart-shaped face look even more inviting. She was beautiful, breathtaking even, and she had no idea just how broken he was.

That was a sobering thought, and Charlie tried hard to shove it down into himself. It did quiet him, however, but luckily it was much harder to notice considering they were going into the movie.

Charlie appreciated the time to collect himself, and it helped that the movie was quite good. Several times he and Daisy laughed aloud, and every so often she would lean over and whisper a comment about the plot. And every time she did, goosebumps would rise along his arm closest to her, and he wasn't sure if he hated the sensation or wanted more of it.

Too bad he never got to quite figure it out, because then the movie was over and they were walking back to the Jeep, ready to ride off to dinner. Charlie mostly listened, if only because Daisy seemed to have a lot to say. From the costumes to the acting, to even how good the score was, it was nice to talk to someone who had no problem expressing just how much they enjoyed something. Charlie couldn't help but feel that Daisy, Clara, and Savannah would have an amazing time having a movie night together.

But that made him think about having Daisy on the ranch again, and all the different reasons he could come up with to invite her. Then *that* sent his mind down a daydream of what it would be like if she was around more often.

"Hey, you okay over there?"

Charlie looked up from where he'd been staring into his milkshake. How long had he been drifting in a fantasy he hadn't even known he had? How embarrassing.

It wasn't like any of that could actually come true. When the rodeo moved on, so would Daisy, and that would be that. She was wonderful, quickly becoming a great friend, even, but she wasn't a permanent fixture. She had a life, and dreams, and Charlie's life was thoroughly rooted in the ranch.

It was *home.*

"Sorry, was just thinking about stuff."

"Heaven forbid. Wouldn't want to do any of that thinking stuff. I hear it gives you ideas."

Grateful for the banter, Charlie rested his chin on his hand and sent her what his sisters called his roguish smile. Personally, he didn't see it. "What kind of ideas?" he asked.

He didn't miss the way her cheeks colored ever so slightly. "That's between you and God, my friend," she replied.

It took every ounce of his power not to sober slightly. There were a lot of things between him and God, and none of them were things he wanted to think about. After all, he was pretty sure the Almighty didn't exactly abide people who broke their vows to him.

But of course, Daisy noticed it, because she straightened. "I didn't mean that to be judgy or anything! I'm pretty sure I believe in the big guy upstairs."

Charlie nodded, waving a hand like it wasn't a big deal. "Don't worry. You didn't come off as judgy."

And suddenly, there were curly fries in front of Charlie's face. "You want to try? They're really good."

It was a completely unsubtle way to change the subject, and

Charlie was grateful. He just wanted to enjoy the moment with Daisy.

But while he was grateful, he didn't expect for her to hold the fry to his mouth until his lips opened, and then she proceeded to hand feed him a long piece.

"See, isn't it good? Crispy on the outside but still nice texture on the inside. I swear, this place has the best curly fries in the state."

She was grinning widely, already picking up another fry and gently holding it to his lips. Charlie opened his mouth again on instinct and carefully took it from her.

It was delicious, sure, but none of his mind registered that. His mind was entirely caught up on just how intimate the moment felt, being hand-fed by someone who just wanted to share something tasty with him.

It felt like every nerve in his body was suddenly alight with a crackling sort of energy. Meanwhile, Daisy was just happily talking about what made a curly fry good or not. She had no idea what she was doing to him, how he was responding to her, and somehow that made his reaction that much more intense.

Time got fuzzy and the connection he felt between them grew. Charlie didn't think he'd ever felt trust increase in real-time, but that was exactly what was happening.

Along with something else... entirely.

Charlie wasn't new to attraction. He'd felt it plenty of times before. But there was a heat in his gut that was spreading out through his body, making his heart beat fast and his mouth go dry. He craved... he craved her *touch*, her attention, he wanted to just be in her presence until he forgot there was a world outside of him.

And despite his normal long list of aversions, the whole idea was *thrilling*.

"Last one," Daisy said casually like she wasn't completely turning Charlie's world inside out.

Just as suddenly as the first fry was offered, the last one was gone. Daisy sat back, wiping her hands, and Charlie chewed, then swallowed. She still seemed to be entirely nonplussed about the whole thing, like it was just a casual exchange between friends.

Then she turned to him, grinning even more broadly. "So, you want to split a dessert?"

CHARLIE HAD BEEN on plenty of dates before his fateful second semester in college, but none of them were like what he experienced with Daisy. He was acutely aware of everything around her, his brain latching on to every minute detail.

Dinner was brilliant and sharing a dessert had been just as simultaneously thrilling and comforting as the fries had been. Charlie didn't realize how touch-starved he'd been, how nice it was to have someone look at him like Daisy did when she offered him a spoonful of cheesecake. Like she was glad that it was him specifically who was there with her, and like his enjoyment of the food was just as delightful to her as actually eating it.

But they couldn't camp at the table all night, much to Charlie's chagrin, and he left a twenty on the table solely for the waitress as an apology for hogging it until almost closing time. Daisy was just as talkative on the ride home, talking about how excited she was for the outfit that Clara was making, and when they finally reached the parking lot, Charlie didn't want her to go.

"Man, this has been the best night I've had in a while," Daisy said, looking out across the couple of rows of trailers with a sigh. "I wish it didn't have to end."

He didn't know how she always seemed to be on the same page as him, but he certainly liked it. "Me too."

She twisted in her seat, giving him an even warmer, broader smile, and that made his brain light up in all sorts of ways. "I'm glad. I'd like to do this again, if you were down."

"Oh, I'm down. I'm so far down that I might actually be in Australia."

It was cheesy, he knew that, but Daisy laughed, nonetheless. Tipped her head back, hands on her stomach, really laughed. It was an amazing sound, and Charlie could easily envision himself getting addicted to it.

"What would—"

He didn't get the words out, but that was probably because Daisy pushed herself up out of her seat and was kissing him.

Daisy Dixon was kissing *him*.

It felt like a thousand things hit him at once, sensations, emotions and desires, but not a single one of them was fear. Charlie's brain short-circuited and all he could think of was how good it felt.

Her hands cupped his face as she continued to kiss him. She was so *warm*, so sweet. He was caught up in her, head spinning, mouth moving against hers like a starving man.

It was electric. It was fire and want and everything he'd thought he could never feel again. The smell of her was in his nose, branding itself into his brain along with everything else about her. He never wanted to let go of the exhilaration. Wanted to drown in it.

"That's it. See, it's not so bad, right?"

That familiar, haunting voice slithered out of his memories, coiling around his ears, and suddenly he was back in *that* place.

"Relax, just have fun with me."

"There you go."

"You're going to remember me forever."

Hands on his body, lips that burned him, condemned his soul. Sensations that overruled his brain and nausea that had him fighting not to get sick all over himself. It was too much! He didn't want... he didn't want...

"Stop!"

Suddenly his hands that had been holding onto Daisy so ardently were pushing her away, shoving her right back into the passenger seat. The world was spinning again, but not in a good way, and Charlie felt like he couldn't *breathe*.

"Whoa, are you okay? Hey, calm down there, Charlie. *Charlie?* Here, I'll open a window."

She reached past him and Charlie flinched away, panic lacing his entire body. He couldn't breathe. He couldn't *breathe*.

"Charlie, I'm sorry if I crossed a line, but I need you to calm down and breathe for me, okay? I'll stay right here on the other side of the Jeep and I won't touch you. I promise."

Her tone was even. Measured. She sounded concerned, but not angry with him. That didn't make sense, and the confusion of it distracted Charlie ever so slightly from the maelstrom inside of him.

Breathe. She just wanted him to breathe. Her hands were raised like one would to show they were unarmed, and her back was pressed into the door, as far away as she could get from him without leaving him alone.

He could still feel her lips on his, the heat of her, the excitement. But the issue was that it wasn't just Daisy's lips. No, there was someone else. Someone he had never wanted to think of again.

"There you go. Your breathing is slowing down. You're safe, Charlie. You're safe and I'm sorry. I never meant to hurt you, and I hope you know that. I'm so, so sorry for getting carried away."

She was... apologizing? She didn't think he was being ridiculous? What kind of grown man went into a panic because of something as simple as a kiss?

It seemed to take an age, maybe even two before he could steadily draw in a breath. He was more embarrassed than he'd ever been in his life. "It's fine," he said raggedly, his throat feeling wrecked. "I just, uh, got startled."

Wow, in the history of unbelievable excuses, that probably had to be in the top ten.

"That's okay. Again, I'm real sorry. I never should have kissed you without permission. That was wrong of me. I was just swept up in how amazing this night was and how happy you looked, and for once I... I just didn't feel so *alone*." Now it was her turn to draw a steadying breath. "But that doesn't matter. I know better. And if you want me to go, I'll go, but I just want to make sure you're safe."

Charlie didn't know what to say. It still felt like his brain was moving through sludge. It still felt like he could feel *her* hands on him. And so, once again, his mouth blurted something out before his mind could think better of it. "Really? That's it?"

She looked hurt, and the whole thing was increasingly making less sense. "What do you mean, that's it? Is there anything else I should apologize for? Because I will. I really, really want you to know that I would never purposefully try to hurt you, Charlie."

He felt like all he could do was stare at her. She was just...

apologizing. Like *she* was the weird one. People didn't just act like that, not when Charlie was acting like a child.

"No, I mean, you're not upset at me? I pushed you away for no reason. You weren't doing anything wrong. You just—" He had to take another breath in, his heart slowly coming down from its painful tempo. "You don't seem angry."

He wasn't expecting her eyes to go wide and her lips to open in a kiss-swollen gasp. She took maybe a half of a second to collect herself, and then she was leaning ever so slightly forward, her tone urgent.

"I have nothing to be angry about. Charlie, you said stop, so we stopped. There's nothing wrong or abnormal about that. And you don't need a reason, ever to say stop." Her words were so genuine, but it was like she was talking another language again. Sure, each individual one had a meaning that made sense, but strung together it just wouldn't translate. "If you have a reason and want to tell me, I am happy to listen. But you owe me *nothing*, Charlie. I want you to understand that. We had a great date, yes, but you. Owe. Me. *Nothing*."

He wanted to listen to her, to believe her, but none of that made sense. "But people don't...You're not going to ask if it's because you're not pretty? Or say something about being a real man? Or even ask me if I like men?"

Because Charlie had tried to be normal, he had. He hadn't just decided one day that the touch of a stranger was going to terrify him to the point where he froze up whenever a woman touched him. He'd tried dating, kissing, even hugging.

And he'd heard a whole lot of things every single time he locked up.

But Daisy just narrowed her eyes at him like *he* was the one who was talking crazy. "Just who are you hangin' with that's telling you those things? I know it can't be your folks on the ranch."

"It's not them. They don't—" He cut himself off. He didn't need to get into that. "Everybody thinks like that, Daisy."

"No, they don't, Charlie. And if anybody says that to you, I will deck them right in their face."

Her vehemence at that last part was so sincere that a surprised laugh barked out of Charlie. "You know what? I believe that."

"Good. I have your back, Charlie. No matter if we never go on a date again, I'm one loyal cowgirl."

Charlie nodded, his tongue coming out to lick his lips. He could taste the mango lip gloss that Daisy had been wearing, and that helped ground him.

"I'm okay now. Thank you."

He couldn't believe how understanding she was being, considering that he'd practically thrown her across the seat. And yet she was acting like it wasn't a big deal. Like he was *normal.*

"I'm glad to hear you're okay. Do you think you're comfortable walking me to my door?"

She still wanted to be by him? It was one thing to be polite to his face; it was another entirely to ask if he would continue to be near her. She should be rushing away, telling him 'thanks for the night' before practically sprinting to her door.

But she wasn't sprinting. No, she was waiting patiently, a soft but slightly sad smile across her pretty face.

"I would like that."

She nodded and turned to her door but didn't open it. Charlie realized after a beat that she was waiting for him to open it for her. She'd seen that it had mattered enough for him to practically race around his car to make sure he got there in time, and she'd changed her habits.

She couldn't be real.

And yet she was. She sat patiently as he got out, went around and did indeed open the door for her. She didn't slide out right away. Instead, her hand cautiously reaching out to hover between them.

Charlie knew what she was doing. She was giving him a silent offer, one that he could turn down without any pressure. One that he could take just as easily. A hand, an extension of support.

So, he took it.

Once more, their hands slid together until their fingers inter-locked. Together, they walked the short distance to Daisy's trailer, the night relatively quiet around them.

"Thank you for the lovely night," Daisy said once they did reach the door of her rusted trailer, turning to look up at him in the moonlight. "I had a good time."

Goodness, she was breathtaking.

"I did too," Charlie murmured, his cheeks still heated from his shame. He was having a hard time believing that what she was saying could possibly be true, and yet her tone was so genuine. "And I would like to do it again sometime."

"Me too."

He was so tired, his head aching from the whiplash of the evening, but there was also a flicker of something else. A sort of faint and fragile... hope, was it?

"I would like to give you a kiss on the cheek," he said finally, swallowing down his fear. "I think I could handle that."

"Are you sure, Charlie? I don't want to do anything that you don't want to. You don't owe me physicality."

"I want to. I'm sure."

"Okay then. I'd like that."

She turned her face so that her cheek was facing him, and he leaned in, pressing his lips to her heated skin. It was quick, it was soft, but it eased the twisting ache inside of him.

"Good night, Charlie," Daisy said when he was done, sending him a smile that some people went entire lifetimes without seeing. Like he was something *special.*

"Good night, Daisy."

She turned, opening her door to head into her place, and Charlie stood there for a long moment. He felt like he was at a crossroads, part of him wanting to go one way while another part of him very much desired to stay rooted exactly where he was, and he had no idea how to navigate either choice.

But one thing was for certain, map or not, he was certainly going to try.

17

Daisy

Daisy was really enjoying dating Charlie.

Sure, things were getting busier and harder as the season progressed, especially when they passed the halfway mark, but that progression in difficulty paled in comparison to how much easier other things were getting.

For one, she was eating a lot more, which was nice. And good meals too. Between the produce that Charlie would bring from home, he would also just show up with lunch for her and remind her of her first rule of life. Daisy didn't mind, of course, and each time she felt a flutter at how happy taking care of her seemed to make him.

And since she rarely had to spend any money on food, she was able to put that toward other things. It wasn't enough to say... turn on her phone, but she was able to pay ten dollars above her minimum payment on her credit card, and actually get some socks without holes in them.

Her phone *did* get paid, however, and that was solely because of all the gas money Charlie was saving her.

Because even though she was still going to AA once a week, he drove her every time. And waited. And then drove her back home. And he always acted like it wasn't a big deal.

Daisy worried occasionally about their budding relationship being entirely too one-sided, but Charlie always acted like her eating meals with him, or sharing a laugh, was a huge deal.

Who knew, maybe to him they were.

Of course, there was the slight, teensy tiny issue of Charlie's dislike of being touched.

Daisy had to adapt to a lot of things in her life, and in truth, she could have rolled with Charlie's aversion if it just seemed like a random quirk. People came in all flavors, and just being in his presence was nice.

But the issue was that his fear didn't seem like a natural thing. No, although she couldn't be sure, it felt like he was legitimately terrified and that something truly awful had made him that way. Her mind would flit off in all sorts of awful directions trying to imagine what had given him practically a phobia of touch.

She didn't want him to be scared around her. And she absolutely wanted to throw hands if someone had hurt him. But it was clear that Charlie had zero desire to discuss why he was the way he was, and she wasn't going to press if he wasn't ready.

But she did desperately want to know. It probably was entirely egotistical, but she felt an overwhelming urge to protect him. To shield him from all the nasty and bitterness in the world until he didn't have to panic at the idea of someone touching him.

"Sooo, I hear that you and Charlie are going on another date tonight?"

Daisy nodded, not even looking up from her phone as Melinda leaned over her. "Mm-hmm."

"You two are getting pretty serious, huh? Funny that you couldn't even stand the guy like three weeks ago."

"Times are a-changin'," Daisy answered without a lick of shame. And what was there to be embarrassed about? She'd disliked Charlie, she'd gotten new info, and she'd changed her opinion. That was that.

"So what're y'all doing on a Sunday night?"

"We're going to that dive diner between here and his town, then I'm going to his ranch to have a movie night with his sister, and I think his niece or something? Then tomorrow I'm going to learn more about the goats and pigs."

"Wow, *spending the night*. And here I thought ol' Charlie boy was one of those squeaky-clean types."

"He is," Daisy responded shortly, her eyes finally flicking up to her friend with dead seriousness. "And it'd be best if you never made a comment about him like that again."

Daisy loved her friend, she did, but she didn't bother to repress the fierce wave of protectiveness that reared up at the comment. It wasn't that she cared if Charlie was virginal or not, or if people thought they'd slept together. No, that didn't matter at all. But she got the feeling that *Charlie* would very much care about such things, and so she wanted to respect that for him, even if he wasn't there.

"Point taken. I hope you have fun though."

"Thank you. I'm fairly certain I will. It's been great so far."

Complicated, but great.

"I'm happy for you, you know that?"

Daisy couldn't help but grin broadly at Melinda, feeling just so *much*. "I do. And I'm happy for me too."

And she meant it.

DAISY'S BELLY was pleasantly full as they drove along to Charlie's ranch. Dinner had been great, and Charlie hadn't blinked twice when she'd asked if they could order two desserts and share them. She felt absolutely spoiled rotten.

Seriously, she'd had both tiramisu and a double fudge cake. And Charlie hadn't even thought it was weird when she took a small scoop of one, a small scoop of the other, and then held up the spoon for him to try.

When she'd first offered him food, the guy had reacted with a strange sort of intensity. At first, she couldn't tell if he was offended or just really weirded out, but he'd kept on eating and had even smiled at one point, so she figured it was fine. And considering how eagerly he agreed to the double dessert idea, she was certain that he didn't mind.

"I hope we're not running too late," she said, looking out the window. Fireflies were just beginning to dot the horizon, giving the flat expanses around them a sort of magical feel. "I know Clara gets to bed pretty early."

"Actually, since she started dating that Nathan guy, she's tended to stay up later. She used to wake up at around four thirty every morning."

"Are you serious?"

"Completely. She's toned it down by waking up around five thirty or six."

"Wow, what a slacker."

"I know, right?"

Daisy chuckled. Sarcasm wasn't Charlie's main form of humor, but she liked when he occasionally dabbled. It kept her on her toes. Humming herself, she leaned against the window and just took it all in. But then she realized that she didn't recognize quite where they were.

"We're going to your ranch, right?"

"We are, but we're going through a back entrance we don't use too often. A new family of ducks recently set up in the back pond that we hardly use, and I thought you'd like to see it."

"Oh! Really? Do they have any hatchlings?"

"You bet they do."

Daisy let out a happy sound that she wasn't even aware that she could make, her feet pattering against the floor.

"But just to warn you, it's late enough that they might all be asleep," he said, not wanting to dampen her enthusiasm but wanting to be realistic.

"That's alright. We can always check it out tomorrow if they are."

"Yeah, that's exactly right."

Sure enough, Charlie turned onto a dirt road that was only *just* visible in the onset of twilight, and a few minutes later they passed a worn fence that looked like it was struggling to stand up.

"I should replace that before winter hits."

Daisy was about to offer to help him, excited to have another excuse to come to the ranch, but then she remembered that she wouldn't be around. By the time Charlie was done helping the rodeo, she would have moved on to the next location that was about another hour and a half southwest of the location they were currently at. And then, she'd go all the way to Cali for a short, two-month stint before the off-season finally hit again.

Huh.

She hadn't thought about that.

She was so wrapped up in all the good that was happening that she'd forgotten to think of the real-world repercussions and limitations. Was she being cruel, pursuing something that couldn't last? And why did the thought of it eventually fading make her feel sick?

She didn't quite like the answer her mind supplied for that, but then the pond came into view and she was able to shove it down into the back of her mind.

It was gorgeous. She felt like she was sneaking into Narnia or some other similarly enchanted place. There was a peaceful sort of hush to the area that beckoned her to come in, to feel the ground on her feet and the night air on her face.

"Let's go."

She forgot to give Charlie a chance to open her door because she was so excited. But he didn't seem to mind, leaning against the car as she took off her shoes.

"What are you doing?"

"I want to feel it on my feet," she replied, not even trying to hide her eagerness. Because what was the point? She liked what she liked, and she wasn't about to hide it. "I want to feel connected."

Daisy recognized that she was being silly, and Charlie would be entirely in the right to tease her about it, but instead he sat right on the ground and started sliding his own boots off.

And she loved that about him.

Putting her shoes into the Jeep so no critter would slip into them while they were gone, she held out her hand to her potential beau. And despite his issues with touching, he always seemed good with that form of physical affection, so she was definitely never going to take that for granted.

Hand in hand, they strolled around the edge, the ground visible in the fading sunlight while the sky began to melt from the soft kiss of lavender into royal blue. It was everything she'd expected the moment that Charlie had mentioned the place, and she felt so centered.

She wished that she could just stay there forever. In the moment, at the pond, on the ranch. She'd been unmoored, following along the rodeo circuit because it was all that she had, but when she was on the Millers' lands, she finally understood what she'd always been looking for.

Too bad she wouldn't ever really belong to it.

"Look, there they are."

Daisy's head jerked in the direction of Charlie's pointed finger and, sure enough, there were a couple of ducks and what seemed like at least a dozen ducklings.

"Oh my gosh!"

It was hard not to hurry over to the edge of the water, but she resisted, knowing that it would likely just scare them off. Because startling or upsetting them seemed like about the worst thing that she could do.

So, she stood there, hand in hand with Charlie, and she was just able to *be*.

It was almost enough to make her cry, but in a good way, like a release of all her tension. It was so easy to envision the future when she was on the ranch, a stretching expanse of endless possibilities that weren't mired in bills or dental work or what she was going to eat. It was just hope and everything that she was willing to dream about.

And she owed it all to Charlie.

Did he know? Probably not. Daisy liked to think that she did a pretty good job of not showing weakness. She was pretty sure he knew she was poor, but probably not how dirt broke she was. After all, the last time she'd had to go shopping before he started his random meal drops, she'd had to decide if she could really afford to buy a toothbrush or if she should wait another week.

But even without knowing, he still did so much for her.

"Charlie?"

"Yeah?" he asked, turning back to her with one of those expressions on his face that made her feel like she was the only woman in the world. Like she could be enough for him. An impossible idea, of course, but that's how he made her feel.

"Could I hug you?"

He waited a moment, which let her know that he was really thinking, not just agreeing because he seemed to feel like he was under some strange obligation to be touchy-feely.

"I'd like that."

She swore her heart swelled with warmth, and she carefully raised her arms. No quick movements, no sudden steps forward. Just a slow, steady approach until he was finally in her arms.

And he felt so *right* there. Warm, strong and solid, his hard-won ranch musculature was an anchor for her, giving her something tangible to hold onto in a world that seemed far too good to be real.

She was content to just stay like that forever, but then Charlie's hands cupped her face and tilted her chin up to look at him. Her brain scrambled to ask what he needed, but she didn't get the question out before his lips were suddenly pressed to hers.

Oh.

Oh, *okay.*

Daisy was down for it, more than down for it, especially since Charlie was the one who started it. Maybe, if he was the one initiating contact, it wouldn't set off his phobia?

That seemed to be the case, because she melted into it, holding on more tightly to him so she wouldn't fly away. Her head rushed and her body called out for *more*.

After all, she was so used to harshness and struggle that whenever something so perfect, so wonderful came along, she just wanted to gobble up as much of it as she could until she split at the seams. More, more, *more*.

She knew that was what got her into trouble, and the exact reason that she was an alcoholic. She just couldn't say no, because she didn't want to. It didn't even occur to her, and every time she found something she liked, she let herself get completely swept away in it without reservations.

So, she clung to him.

Her blood was rushing, her heart thundering, and her mind racing to all that *could* be. She wanted to know everything she could about him, to inscribe everything about him into her memory until she could recite it in her sleep.

But then something was... off.

His hands began to shake. And then the kiss grew more desperate, almost terrified, and for the first time in her life, Daisy said no to what she wanted.

"Hey, Charlie. *Charlie!*" She broke away, lifting her hands to rest on his shoulders. She stared up at his face, trying to search for what was going on. "I need you to check in with me. Are you okay?"

He blinked at her like he wasn't quite sure what she was saying, but then suddenly he was falling to her knees, clinging to her while his breath came in jagged, rapid little gasps.

"Charlie, you're scaring me. I need you to breathe again, okay?"

But *he'd* been the one to kiss her. She had respected his boundaries entirely. *He* was the one to push it.

Sliding down to her knees, she took his hands in hers. "Just breathe with me, okay? In, then out. Nice and slow. You're okay. You're home and we're at the pond you were showing me, remember?"

"I don't understand how you can just stand there and act like this is normal."

"Technically, I'm kneeling."

Apparently that was the wrong thing to say, because Charlie just hung his head, a sob wracking his body. "What kind of man can't even kiss the woman he's in love with."

"Charlie—"

Wait.

What?

It was so tempting to let herself linger on what he'd said. That he'd dropped the "L" word. But that would have been far too selfish, so she shoved that back with the deluge of thoughts that came along with that and focused solely on Charlie.

"You're not any less of a man because you have a touch aversion. There's nothing wrong with that," Daisy murmured, carefully reaching up, trying to telegraph what she was doing. "So just breathe for me, okay?"

Fortunately, he did indeed do that. His gasping slowed down, although it still sounded very wet. The idea that Charlie was crying because he was ashamed of his aversion made her heart truly ache.

"I'm so sorry, Daisy. I just wanted to be able to hold you."

"It's okay, Charlie. Really, if you're only able to hold my hand,

I'm okay with that. I like *you,* quirks and all. *But...*" She hesitated, wondering if she was passing a boundary she couldn't come back from, but she had to know. "I can't help but feel like this phobia comes because there's something inside of you that's hurting you. Something that maybe, it would help you to talk about."

He didn't answer at first, just breathing raggedly, and when he finally raised his head, Daisy's breath caught in her throat. He looked in pain, like someone had stabbed him and ripped his heart out.

"You don't want to know."

"No, Charlie, I do. But only if you want to tell me."

He swallowed as her thumbs stroked away the tears that were streaking down his handsome face. His handsome, tortured face.

"I can do that."

18

Charlie

He was too full of everything. Emotions, terror, memories, sensation. They all rushed through him, filling him up to the brim until he was sure that he was going to pop. He wanted to sink into the floor. He wanted to disappear forever. But with Daisy's hands on his face and that impossibly kind expression on her features, he felt like maybe, maybe he could fulfill her request. That maybe he could speak the evil that'd been feeding in his soul for nearly a decade.

"I was a freshman in college."

Just a sentence, and a rather simple one at that, but uttering it made something break within him and he was plunged back down in the darkness.

"Charlie, come back to me. You're home. You're at the Miller Ranch, okay?"

Somehow, Daisy was able to bring him back, to draw him back up to the surface. He didn't realize at first that he was crying again, even harder than the first time.

"It's okay. You don't have to tell me a thing if it hurts you that much."

But he'd already ripped the band-aid off and all that darkness wanted to escape. "No, no. I need to keep going." He swallowed, internally cursing that he didn't have a hanky in his pocket. Didn't Papa say to always carry a hanky? "It was college. I went to a party. I was supposed to go with Raph, but he got really sick the day before."

He could still see it in his mind's eye. There'd been this cute redhead in his public speaking class who was supposed to be there, and he wanted to see if he could maybe give her a kiss or two before the night was over.

"It was going well at first, but then this sorority girl took an interest in me. She was pretty, with long brunette hair and these honey doe eyes. I thought I was pretty much as lucky as I could be."

He remembered flirting with her, preening like a peacock. He was an idiot.

"She got me this fancy foreign lager at first. I wasn't opposed to drinking a little, so I had no problem emptying it over an hour or so. But then she made me this mixed drink. I wasn't into liquor, not really, but she looked so hurt that I didn't even want to try. So, I drank that too.

"And once that was gone, she gave me another. I told her I didn't want another one, but she insisted, and so I drank that too."

He risked a glance to Daisy and, although she was listening intently, she looked absolutely horrified. And she should have been, because Charlie could feel the evil oozing out of his mouth, born from what had happened to him.

"I lost track of the drinks, and it didn't take long for me to be drunk. *Too* drunk. Drunker than I'd ever been in my life. It's hard to remember exactly what happened after that. But she took me by the hand, and led me upstairs, and then…"

His mouth was dry. His hands were shaking. He felt like he was going to be sick, but he still kept going.

"I woke up with her on top of me, on a bed. She kept telling me that she was helping me, that she was going to make me a real man. I was too drunk to realize what was happening. I could barely keep my eyes open."

Daisy audibly gasped, and suddenly he was pulled to her, her arms wrapped strongly around him. "Charlie, I'm so sorry! I'm just—" Her voice cracked, and suddenly she was crying too. "You didn't deserve that. Nobody deserves that."

Once again, her reaction didn't make sense. She was supposed to ask why he was upset. After all, all men loved sex, right?

But she didn't say anything like that. Instead, she just held him.

Charlie stayed still, reeling. He was overwhelmed by all the memories that he had been suppressing for years, but at the same time he was completely baffled by the woman sitting next to him.

Eventually, she pulled away just enough to look up at his face. "What happened? Did you report her? Is she in jail?"

Numbly, Charlie shook his head. "Nothing happened to her. I went to the campus police, but when I tried to report her, they brushed me off. They didn't believe me. That something like that could happen to me." He remembered how the officer had looked him in the eye and said he was bigger and stronger than any girl on campus, so how had he let a tiny cheerleader manhandle him? He'd sat there, fingernail marks down his chest, hickey still on his neck, and no one cared.

"What? Are you kidding me? That's crazy. I hope your Papa sued their pants off."

"I never told my family."

She didn't say anything, her jaw literally hanging open for a moment before she gathered herself enough to speak. "You didn't tell them?"

"No. No one knows except for her, me and the campus police officers who never believed me."

"Charlie, my dear, that's not healthy for you. You were assaulted. And you need to talk about it to someone. Your therapist, a pastor, your father. You need the support of the people you trust the most."

"How could I ever tell them?" Charlie snapped, more out of desperation rather than anger.

"What do you mean? Don't you think they'd want to know? That they'd want to comfort you in your time of need?"

"How could I ever look in my father's face after admitting that I broke my vow I made to God?"

"Broke your... Charlie, I don't understand. Can you explain to me?"

Could he explain? He probably couldn't stop if he tried. It was like the words were punching themselves out of his face after being bottled up for nearly seven years. "I vowed to save myself for marriage, and it's something all of my sisters have kept. I destroyed my marriage bed before even getting there by a woman half my size! I—" His voice broke again and he sank into his misery. He was such a failure. Sure, there wasn't any sort of physical sign of virginity, but it had been an oath between him and God, a promise. And he'd lost that because he'd let himself be weak.

"Charlie, are you telling me you think that you've disappointed God because you were raped?"

"Stop saying that. I wasn't... I *wasn't*—"

Her hands were suddenly on his face again, cool and soothing.

"Charlie Miller, sugar, you didn't break your oath to God." That stopped his growing frenzy just about as fast as it had started, and he found himself staring at her in shock.

"How is that even remotely possible? I had sex."

"No. No, you didn't. Now, I've never really been into this whole virginity thing, but from what I understand, you made an oath to God that you would choose to sleep with your future spouse and only your future spouse."

"Yeah, that's generally how it goes."

"You didn't choose to sleep with anyone, Charlie. Yes, that woman did something she should never have done. She took away an experience from you that should have been beautiful and made it into something dark. But if you believe for a second that God would condemn you for someone hurting you so deeply, then we're familiar with two very different big guys in charge."

Could that possibly be true?

Charlie had always believed that virginity was more of a spiritual concept. To him, the body wasn't where the promise was. It was in the heart.

So, if he'd never given his heart to his attacker. If he'd never *wanted* to... what if Daisy was right?

But all the shame bubbled up, whispering everything in his ears that he'd heard whenever a male victim was brought up.

"You don't think I'm less of a man for it? That I should have fought her off?"

"What? No! And anyone who tells you that has no idea what they're talking about."

She leaned in close and somehow, Charlie wasn't afraid. He was upset, he was ashamed, he was flabbergasted and maybe more than a bit lost. But he wasn't afraid.

He didn't know if he could ever be afraid of Daisy.

"She got you drunk and took advantage. You trusted her, because you're a kind person and you never imagined that someone would be so cruel. You are a *man,* Charlie Miller, an amazing man who is kind, caring, and frankly hilarious.

"If I could go back in time and beat the tar out of this woman, I would. But I know it doesn't work like that, so all I can do is be here for you right now, in this moment, and tell you it's not your fault. None of this is your fault.

"You didn't break your oath, Charlie. And I'm sure if God is watching, he'd be so proud of all the things you've done. How you didn't let that woman's bad deeds corrupt you. You're *amazing,* in every sense of the word."

There was no way she could mean all that. And yet, when he looked into her beautiful eyes, he only saw the truth there. Truth and a whole lot of pain.

How could he not believe her when she looked at him like *that.*

The tears came again, and they sat there holding each other, squeezing so tightly that he was surprised that she didn't creak. He loved her, it was so soon, but he knew he could search the entire world and never find another like Daisy Dixon.

So he just let himself hold her while he thought about every-thing that he had been through. He thought about the innocence he had lost before he had wanted to. He thought about the need-less hate he put himself through. He thought about all the other people in the world who have gone through things like this.

And now, for the first time since he'd woken up that horrible night so long ago, he felt like maybe, just maybe, one day he could share intimacy with someone and not be overcome with panic.

It was dark by the time they loosened their holds on each other.

"Are you ready to go home?" she asked, voice quiet and sounding utterly wrecked. And as much as he hated knowing she'd been so upset, he couldn't help but feel amazed that she felt that way about *him.*

"Actually... I would like to talk about it more. That is, if you want to listen."

Strange, how he'd avoided ever mentioning anything about it for year after year, keeping it a secret from even his family, but now that it was out, there was so much that he wanted to say. So much he needed to mourn, so much he needed to be angry over.

Daisy leaned in close, not quite kissing him, but gently touching her forehead to his. "I'll always be willing to listen to whatever you're willing to tell me."

He couldn't have asked for anything more.

19

———————

Daisy

"Alright, stay still. I just need to put a couple of temporary pins in."

"Just don't poke me. I'd hate to get blood on this brand-new outfit."

"I appreciate you pretending that this isn't going to get absolutely filthy out there in the arena, but I promise I won't poke you as long as you don't move."

"Point taken."

Daisy's arms were starting to ache from where she was holding them up like an airplane, but she tried to stay as still as she could. It was strange to be standing in the middle of Clara's workroom, fabric and materials all around her. The mirrors in front of her were covered, apparently to make sure Daisy didn't see her new outfit in its entirety until Clara was ready.

But even looking down at herself, Daisy couldn't believe that this was really happening.

The truth was that most female riders didn't wear anything much different than male riders, wanting to be respected and seen as no different than their counterparts. But Daisy's figure was far too curvy to hide it, and she loved to wear her long thick hair free just as much as she loved having it tied back. Sure, it made everything more complicated, but she found a power in her femininity. She remembered struggling with being taken seriously at first because of it, so she'd decided to just lean into it. Go whole-hog.

Which was just about the most Daisy thing she could do, really.

She'd started with electric blue, fringed chaps and a neon pink shirt with black shoulders. She remembered making quite an impression when she first rode into the ring, and not a good one. The audience was almost silent, some of their groans audible. They thought she was just a chunky barbie who didn't belong there. A diversity hire.

So, when she'd completed the barrel course in incredible time, then spent another three minutes doing show tricks with her mount, including a mounted bow and even laying down, the crowd went wild. That was when she'd learned that getting their expectations real low made her look all the more impressive when she showed them what she could do.

After that, she remembered spending three dollars on rhinestones online and eagerly waiting for them to be delivered to the rodeo. When they finally were, she stayed up all night and rhinestoned one of her three outfits until they were all gone, and when the glue finally cured, she wore it to her next shift.

She had felt *amazing*. Like a sparkling jewel and one of a kind.

The audience had laughed at first, no doubt sure that she was some sort of joke act, and she'd left them with their jaws on the ground amongst the rhinestones she lost because she hadn't glued them down quite as much as she needed to.

So that had become her schtick, and she became known for it. But rodeo work wasn't exactly easy on outfits, and she never managed to have more than three at a time, even when she tried to make sure she repaired them whenever they were damaged.

The idea that her wardrobe was about to increase was mind-boggling to her, especially since Clara clearly hadn't held anything back.

First of all, Daisy had expected to wear her dark jeans under whatever the seamstress had created, but nope, the woman had handed her a pair of slacks made out of a thick but softer fabric, telling her that those were a part of her base along with a thin, cotton tank top before pointing to the bathroom.

Daisy had put them on, and by the time she was out of the bathroom, Clara had pulled out of nowhere a mint-colored top with pink shoulders, delicate-looking flowers embroidered on it and dusted with rhinestones.

Then there were the matching chaps that went with it. The fringe on them was ridiculously long, which was perfect, and the rivets looked like they were *actually diamond*. It was too much, and for a moment Daisy hadn't been able to speak. But then Clara was picking something off her sewing table and holding up a jacket that was just *far* too incredible.

It was also pink, with rhinestones around the pockets, the seams and everywhere else one might expect. But that wasn't it. Even in the blank spaces, tiny little stones laid in delicate filigree, twisting this way and that until it refracted rainbows all over the workroom.

But that wasn't it either. The fringe, which hung long on the arms and shorter on the torso where it would get more in the way, wasn't dyed suede or hide. No, it was actual rhinestone chains, sparkling brightly enough to look like they just might be Swarovski.

Still, it was one thing to see the outfit in front of her, another to see it when she looked down, and even another to see it all put together in the mirror. So, although she was trying her best to be patient, she really did want to look at her reflection.

"Alright, are you ready?"

"I've been ready since the moment I saw the first sparkle."

"That's the attitude I like to hear. Now close your eyes and don't open until I say so."

Daisy slammed her eyes shut, excitement bubbling in her gut. It seemed to take forever for Clara to give the cue, but when she did, Daisy's eyes practically slammed open.

And she wasn't disappointed.

"Oh, my goodness," Daisy said, mindful to watch her language around the middle Miller child. "It's *gorgeous*."

"You like it?" Clara asked, her grin looking like it could practically split her face. "Yay! I was so worried."

"How could I not like it? Clara, this is *perfect*."

Daisy was perfectly aware of the fact that some people would find the outfit gaudy. Over the top. Tacky. But the thing about Miss Scarlet was that she was unapologetically all those things. She shined brighter than anyone thought she should and won them over in the end anyways. She *demanded* attention even if they didn't want to give it, which made it even more satisfying when they realized she was actually good at what she did.

And maybe it was a little egotistical, but Daisy liked to think that just maybe there was some little future cowgirl in the audience that would see her looking like a beautifully personified version of a disco ball and realize she could do that too if she wanted.

"Wow, Clara. You've outdone yourself."

Daisy nearly jumped out of her own skin, whirling to see Charlie leaning in the doorway, his eyes scanning her from head to toe. The fringe was so long that it dramatically *swooshed* after her, and the back of her mind couldn't help but notice the movement. It was going to look amazing on horseback, flouncing this way and that when she leapt over a barrel.

"I think I can confidently say I agree with you," Clara said with a nod. "Do us a spin, Daisy. Would you?"

Like she would ever refuse a request like that. Daisy spun one way, then the other, then struck a model pose with a flourish.

"I absolutely love it," Daisy exclaimed. "This one going to be one show stopping get-up!"

"I guess we're lucky to see it before the show then," Charlie murmured and *oh wow,* if there wasn't a lot to his tone. It reminded her of how he looked when he'd kissed her, before he'd fallen apart, and she flushed.

"Well then," Clara said, clearing her throat. "I think we just need the hat now."

Daisy's eyebrows shot right up to her hairline. "Clara, you didn't."

But the tall woman put on an innocent look that totally didn't fool Daisy. "Okay, I hear where you're coming from. But what if... I did?"

"Clara, it's too much."

But the woman was already hurrying over to another door that Daisy hadn't even gone through, disappearing with the click of her heels. Daisy looked uncertainly to Charlie, but he just gave a resigned shrug.

"Clara's gonna be Clara. This kind of stuff is in her blood. Just go along for the ride."

Well, if the woman was going to insist on draping Daisy in hand-tailored finery, she wasn't going to protest. She couldn't remember the last time she'd been so welcomed, made to feel so important.

"Ta-da."

Clara emerged with a pink cowboy hat in her hands, also rhinestoned, but the material itself was embossed with golden roses that made it look like the highest end brocade that Daisy had ever seen.

She remembered drooling over videos or articles online that featured other 'glam' cowboys and cowgirls, wishing that she could have even one item as nice as them. But now, she had an entire outfit that she could never have afforded otherwise.

"Oh, *Clara.* It's beautiful." Daisy felt big tears well up in her eyes, and she didn't even try to hide them. She was just too happy.

But it wasn't just because she had a fancy outfit. It was because Clara had taken so much time out of her very busy life to painstakingly craft something just for Daisy. She didn't have to, and Daisy certainly hadn't asked her to, but she'd done it because she *wanted* to. Because she thought Daisy was worth all the effort. That Daisy *deserved* to wear something so amazing.

It was so *much.* Much more than she ever thought was possible.

"Hey, you okay?" Charlie asked, his voice layered with concern.

"I'm okay," Daisy said, grinning so hard her cheeks hurt.

"More than okay. Thank you, Clara. You don't know how much this means to me." And then she *really* burst into tears, feeling so welcome, so loved, that it couldn't help but well up out of her eyes and down her cheeks.

"Oh, my darling," Clara said, crossing over to her and enveloping Daisy in a hug. It was a lovely, warm hug, and she didn't pull away until the cowgirl stopped crying. "You're a real gem. My brother wouldn't be spending so much time with you if you weren't."

Clara pulled a handkerchief from her utility belt around her waist and dabbed at Daisy's face. The sheer sweetness and motherliness of the act made her chuckle, however.

"Goodness, I'm a mess, aren't I?"

"Maybe," Charlie said with a grin from where he was standing. "But you're the prettiest mess I've ever seen."

That made Daisy flush and she glanced back to Clara, expecting her to tease them about the mild flirting, but instead the woman just looked... guilty? Why would she look guilty?

And then it came...

"Soooo..." Clara said slowly, tucking her handkerchief back in her pocket. "Should I wait to bring out the boots, or do you think you've recovered enough for that?"

"*Clara!*"

20

—————

Charlie

Charlie took a long gulp of the soda he'd bought from the vending machine. Normally he wasn't much for sugary drinks, but after the hour he'd just had, he could use the pick-me-up.

But, as exhausted as he was, he was glad he'd actually done what Daisy suggested and got a therapist. It wasn't his first time, of course. After Mama died, Papa had made sure to get all of them into an office to deal with their grief. But even that might not have happened if Cici hadn't suddenly been stricken with constant panic attacks and night terrors.

While Clara and Cass had kept up with it, Charlie had let it fall to the wayside when he'd been halfway through high school. He definitely should have gone back after *the event,* as he was calling it, but going to a therapist felt like admitting that he'd actually gone through trauma, and he was in such denial that it had always stopped him from ever setting up an appointment.

Taking another lengthy gulp, he screwed the cap on and headed outside. He'd parked down the road at a garage, but he was surprised to see a familiar face waiting outside on the sidewalk for him.

"Daisy?" he asked. "What are you doing here?"

But she just grinned and held up a bag of tortilla chips along with a jar that must have been that salsa she talked about making. "You wait for me outside of AA. I can wait for you outside of therapy."

"What about the extra shift you were picking up?"

"I already finished it. I had permission to clock in at four and work until noon. Took a nap, and now I'm here."

Charlie looked behind her to see her old, rusted truck. How much gas money had she spent just to see him? He wasn't 100% privy to her financial situation, but he wasn't naïve enough to not know how expensive it was to make frivolous trips in her old gas-guzzling vehicle.

"You didn't have to do that."

"I know." She strode forward and offered her hand. Charlie took it, thrilled that she still wanted to touch him.

They hadn't kissed again since the pond, but Charlie had realized that although part of him very much wanted to be able to, he just wasn't at that level yet. And Daisy seemed perfectly alright with that.

It still boggled his mind when he thought about it. He expected eye rolls at his story, or comments about him being whiny. Pathetic. But he never saw so much as a hint of that in her face. Only support and trust.

She was amazing.

"Hey, I saw what looked like a really good food cart by a park near here. Want to walk there and pig out on junk food?"

"That sounds perfect."

They strolled the couple of blocks there, but not before Charlie topped up the parking meter. Daisy assured him that she didn't need him to, but he wasn't about to have her use her own quarters after coming all the way to keep him company.

There was a line to the cart, but it went pretty quickly, and it ended up with her getting a gyro, him getting souvlaki and them sharing some falafel and baklava.

It was quite a lot to try to carry as they hunted down a bench or a picnic table, but eventually they did find one and spread out their banquet.

"So, how did therapy go?"

"Well, it was an intake meeting so I was just explaining why I was there and what I was hoping for. You know, groundwork stuff."

"That makes sense. I hope you know that I think it's amazing how fast you found a therapist. I know that's not an easy step to take."

"Do you?"

"Charlie, I'm a recovering addict. I probably wouldn't have ever gotten to the actual recovery part if my old insurance hadn't covered multiple appointments with a rehabilitation therapist."

"Oh, I never knew you went."

"That's fine. But in my opinion, everyone should get free therapy. It's like a public health service, really. I probably would have caused a lot less chaos if I'd gotten help earlier."

There was a story there, and Charlie wanted to ask about it. He felt like Daisy knew so much of his past, but he knew so little of hers. Where were her parents? Were they passed like his

Mama? Did she miss them? Why did she never talk about them? How had she become an alcoholic? How did she realize that she was?

But he didn't get to ask a single one before she was talking again. "When do you think you're going to tell your family?"

Charlie stiffened at that. He didn't know why, but he hadn't expected that particular question. "I don't really know."

He was working on listening to what Daisy had said about his oath to God. He was working on not viewing himself as a failure of a man. But just because *he* was working on that didn't mean that his family would see him that way. But the thought of even the *remote possibility* of them seeing him in a different light made him sick to his stomach.

His family was his whole life. He loved the ranch, loved his siblings. He loved the community that they were making. The idea of losing it because they didn't think like Daisy did was terrifying. But really, he should know better than that. His family wasn't that way.

"I don't want them to think I failed them."

Daisy reached over, squeezing his hand. He didn't know when they'd gotten so touchy, but he was immensely grateful for it. "They won't, I promise. Your family is just like you. They'll be heartbroken, and they'll want to be there for you."

"That's easy for you to say. They're not your family." Charlie grumbled, then regretted he said it at all.

But Daisy just gave him a sad smile. "No, it's easy for me to say because my mother hated me, and I know your family is the exact opposite of anything she ever was."

Oh.

21

Daisy

Most days, Daisy woke up ready to tackle the day and actually looking forward to what was in store for her. She never could have imagined that her life could have turned in the direction that it had, but she was immensely grateful.

She was shocked and horrified at what had happened to Charlie in college, and she felt incredibly guilty that she had ever judged him for his need for space. But she was also immensely proud about all the steps he was taking.

He'd gone from a sobbing mess who clearly hated himself, who blamed himself for everything, to someone who was actively working on his trauma. He went to therapy weekly. He used better language in regard to himself. And he took Sundays off his schedule so he could go to his church back home.

Daisy was so happy that Charlie was taking that time for himself, because it edified him. She hoped that he was talking to his pastor and congregating with other members who were important to him. Because the pain that had been in his voice when he'd talked about how he'd somehow failed God had been so utterly awful.

Daisy didn't believe for a minute that Jesus or His Father would ever punish a victim for something like that. If anything, they would be rooting for that person to heal, to recover. Daisy didn't get why they'd let it happen in the first place, but that question was a slippery slope she'd learned not to try to climb on.

So the days passed, Charlie kept going to therapy, Daisy kept attending her AA meetings, and she spent just about every other rodeo-weekend on the ranch.

It was wonderful. She would even dare to say that it was perfect. It was certainly more than she ever dreamed of. But the thing about time passing was that it was actually *passing*, which meant their time at their first location was almost to an end.

And that scared her.

She didn't want to lose Charlie. And although she was moving an hour and a half away along with the rodeo, she didn't want things to end. She was scared of the issue, but she knew that she couldn't keep avoiding it. Avoidance was one of the easiest habits to fall into, and sliding into that made it easier to slide into other things she had no business sliding into.

Because, as it were, she was nearly three months sober. She couldn't wait to get that chip again, and she was going to keep it right under her pillow. She'd certainly earned it because it hadn't been easy.

Most of the time she never felt the compulsion to drink. But when Charlie was having an especially bad day, or when she thought back to that night when he'd finally told her the origin of his phobia, it was real tempting to glug-glug until her heart stopped feeling like it was shattering.

It just wasn't fair. It was just so *wrong.*

Daisy didn't live under a rock. She understood what toxic masculinity was and how it taught men that they could never be weak. Could never be vulnerable. She'd even watched the news where reports of a female teacher assaulting a male student were met with jokes instead of the horror that it deserved.

So, she got why Charlie was scared of anyone knowing. He clearly took great pride in his faith and his image as a Miller. Daisy really wished she could take a baseball bat to that campus officer who dismissed him, and she prayed every single night that the woman didn't go on to hurt anybody else.

"You look like you're thinking about something awful."

Daisy jumped, realizing she'd stopped in the middle of tossing hay and was just staring into the distance. She seemed to be doing that a lot more often, but her life certainly seemed to be full of a lot more things to think about.

"Oh, hey Rick. I was thinkin' some pretty serious thoughts."

"I hope I'm not interrupting, but I was kinda hopin' to ask you something?"

She turned to face the man fully. He was a tall, lanky fellow. Cute, in a country sort of way. He was missing two of his teeth from, if she remembered right, a kick from a donkey when he was a kid, but somehow it didn't detract from his welcoming sort of presence. He was awkward, maybe even a touch dopey, but the moment he got into the ring he moved with confidence, flow, and almost a sense of grace.

"What can I help you with, sugar?"

His cheeks began to blush a light pink. "I hope I'm not over-stepping, Daisy, but I've always been so impressed by you in the ring and how you treat the animals. Now, I missed a chance with a lovely lady because I was too nervous to ever step up, so I figured if I wanted things to be different, I needed to put my neck out."

Oh, wait, was he—

"So, I was wondering, would you want to get a cup of coffee sometime?"

Poor, sweet Rick. He really was a lovely guy, and maybe if she hadn't met Charlie, she'd be game. "Aww, that's super sweet of you. But I'm sorry, I'm seeing someone."

"You are? Oh, I'm sorry. I didn't mean to overstep."

"It's okay. Neither of us talk about it much. But I appreciate it, and I think it's really cool that you stuck your neck out."

"Really? It don't come across as desperate?"

Daisy shook her head. "No, cause you were honest, and you listen. If you'd laid down some sort of lie, it probably would have. But hey, if I meet any ladies I think could use a tall cowboy, I'll introduce you."

"That's mighty kind of you, Miss Daisy. You sure do make a fella feel better about a no."

"Hey, I aim to please."

He chuckled, then grabbed his own pitchfork and started tossing hay with her. What a lovely gentleman. "It wouldn't be too nosey to ask who the lucky man is, would it? I understand if you're private and don't want to, but... well, I guess I'm more like a cat than I thought."

Daisy couldn't help but chuckle at that. Not because it was particularly funny, but because her mind instantly imagined the man in a Halloween catsuit and that was pretty amusing.

"I don't mind sharing, because I trust you. It's Charlie."

"Charlie? As in Charlie Miller?"

"Do you know any other Charlies around here?"

"Fair enough." There was a lull and they both continued tossing hay until Rick spoke again. "Is he coming with us to the next location then?"

Of course, he would ask that.

"I don't actually know."

"Well, you best step on that girl. If you guys are fine with the distance, that's between the two of you. But you better make sure the both of you are on the same page if you're serious."

"Ugh, you know what, Rick? When you're right, you're right."

He beamed at her, all boyish charm and genuine friendship. "Hey, you know what they say about broken clocks."

"You're not broken," Daisy objected out of habit. "You're just uniquely designed."

"Uniquely designed?" She didn't think it was possible, but his grin grew even wider. "Now I like how that sounds. But don't think you distracted me. You got a serious conversation ahead of you."

"Yeah, don't remind me."

22

Charlie

"Will you tell me if this tastes better with the pure tomato sauce or the barbeque sauce?"

Charlie looked up from his phone, in the middle of texting Daisy. It was one of the weekends where she stayed at the rodeo and picked up extra shifts. He wished that she didn't have to do that, but even with the twenties that he kept sneaking into her laundry, she still said she needed the extra hours. He'd like to find a way to put hundreds around her place, but he figured that would be a bit *too* obvious.

But Clara looked thoroughly amused. "Ooooh, are you texting your lady friend?"

"*Lady friend*?" Charlie parroted. "What, are we in middle school?"

"Come on, don't dodge the question. What's she saying? Does she want another outfit?"

"*Clara*, of course Daisy wouldn't want another outfit. She's immensely grateful for the last one, and you know that she's worried about seeming like she's taking advantage of people."

"Oh."

"So of course you should make her another outfit."

She clapped her hands and made a series of happy noises that could only be described as Clara-isms. "Yes! I was hoping you'd say that. You scared me for a minute."

"Well, I know she would tell you no, but I'm sure she'll love it."

"I can't wait to get started! I've already got a color scheme in mind for her next outfit. It's going to look so good."

Charlie shook his head and then reached for the two small plates that she'd pushed toward him. "What kind of sauces are these again?"

"Tomato and Barbeque."

He tasted one and then the other, then realized that it was some sort of meatloaf, but there was something different about it. He knew better than to ask, however, unless he wanted to end up in a half-hour explanation of her latest culinary experiment.

"Sooooooo," Clara began in a sing-song tone that told him that she probably wasn't about to ask about the food she'd just given him. "What's going on with you and Miss Daisy, my favorite rodeo performer?"

"I'm pretty sure she's the only rodeo performer you know."

"That doesn't make my point any less accurate."

"I think it does."

"Ugh, is this dodgeball or a conversation? I swear, all little brothers take an absurd amount of pleasure in being needlessly pedantic."

"Right, because you definitely have a plethora of experience to pull from given you have so many little brothers."

"*Charlie!* Come on, you're killing me. I need the deets. Are you two going steady? Are you in an exclusive relationship? Are you in *looove*?" She said the last word in a hopeless sigh and basically melted into a puddle across the counter. Charlie loved his sister, he did, but he didn't always get all of her eccentricities. One of them being how she looked at life through romance-colored glasses.

"I mean... we're dating."

"Believe it or not, I gathered that much," she said, instantly sobering. "But come on, the season is almost over and she'll be moving on, so surely you've got some sort of plan for what the two of you are going to do."

Whoops.

Charlie froze midchew, his mind realizing that he may have just maybe forgotten to do something very important. But with everything on his plate, time had just been moving so fast.

"You *do* know what the two of you are going to do... right?"

Yeah, definitely a big whoops.

Charlie took his time finishing chewing, and when he swallowed, it felt like a rock going down his throat. "I may or may not have been putting off that talk."

"Charlie Miller, do you mean to tell me that you haven't nailed things down with the first woman you've shown interest in since you were nineteen years old?"

"I don't see why it's that big of a deal. We'll work something out."

"Work something out? Your girl is about to move another

hour and a half away on top of the forty-five minutes that she's already away and your time with the rodeo is gonna stop. That's a huge transition and decrease in time together, and you're acting like you don't care. Don't you think that's gotta make her feel really unvalued? I know that if Nathan suddenly completely changed our schedule and made no effort to find time for us that I'd be pretty wounded."

"I just have a lot on my plate, okay, Clara?"

"And what on that plate could be more important than securing the possible love of your life?"

"This isn't one of your old movies, Clara. Not everything is all roses and happy endings like that."

"Well, it certainly isn't going to be if you keep procrastinating. Chop-chop, brother."

Rolling his eyes, Charlie got up from the table. It was far too early in the morning to be lectured by his next-oldest sibling. "I'm going to go for a ride. I'll see you later, Clara."

"Avoidance will get you nowhere, Charlie."

"I'll see you at lunch, Clara."

He didn't let the door slam on the way out—he was raised better than that—but the temptation was there. It wasn't that he disagreed with Clara, but the sudden realization that he was running out of time had startled him, put him off-kilter, and he found the anxiety that had been waning the past few weeks rising right back up again.

Why did everything have to be so complicated?

He wished that he could just be a normal person, that he could hold and kiss Daisy like anyone else. That he didn't have to see a therapist every single week just to learn how not to fall to pieces at the thought of intimacy.

But he couldn't have any of that. He'd been wounded, deeply, had someone use him in a way that no one was meant to be used without consent. And then he'd hid it, letting the shame and that woman's evil ruminate in him, hidden in a dark corner that grew, and grew, and grew until even kissing the woman that he was madly in love with made him spiral into a dark place.

Because he knew, without a doubt, that he was in love with Daisy.

He knew it was soon, that just two months earlier he hadn't wanted anything to do with her. But that was before he'd gotten to know the real her. When he'd let his perception of her, as well as her dislike of him, influence him.

Because Miss Daisy Dixon was one of the kindest, bravest women he knew. She hadn't been handed an easy life. She was poor, she clearly didn't have family, and she struggled with addiction. But she got herself to AA. She asked him for help when she really needed it. She helped everyone around her and she *listened.*

Charlie had told her his greatest secret. What he'd been hiding and protecting for years.

And she'd told him it wasn't his fault.

He still struggled with that idea, of course. It was what he and his therapist worked on the most. But it was like her uttering the phrase unlocked a possibility in his mind that he had never dared to think about. He'd always blamed himself because he should have been stronger, shouldn't have let himself be tricked, should have fought harder. That if he was a *real* man, he never would have allowed something like that to happen to himself. Or, that maybe he wasn't a real man, because he *didn't* want that to happen to him, like many men did.

And just like that, she'd offered him a different path.

He didn't want to lose that.

But he also didn't want to scare Daisy off by being too clingy.

Because she was amazing, she really was. Whenever she was on the ranch, he found himself wishing that those days would last forever. When he brought her lunches, he wished those could last forever too. But he also didn't want to be a stage five clinger by telling her that the idea of her leaving, of being even farther away from him, made him miserable.

"I've really gotten myself into a pickle, haven't I?"

The horses stabled around him didn't agree or disagree, but when he approached the closest one, he couldn't help but feel like that it understood him.

Either that or the big guy wanted a treat, but Charlie preferred the first option.

"It's been a while since I've been here, hasn't it?"

Thankfully Mick had taken over most of the horse responsibilities, and Charlie didn't mind because he was *good* at it. Not that it was a surprise considering how well-trained and basically perfect Othello was. But he missed their tiny little herd, and it was high time he rode again.

Despite his long absence, he was able to get his chosen mount all saddled up and outside fairly expeditiously. In his mind, it was because the horses missed him as much as he missed them.

But again... it was probably the whole treat thing.

Oh well, Charlie didn't mind that he ranked slightly below an apple. After all, the fruits were pretty delicious.

It felt good to be on the back of a horse again, even if he was just riding around the rarely used path around the edge of their land. Although he wasn't a trick rider by any means, not like Daisy, he still loved the freedom and power of sitting atop a horse, feeling the muscle beneath him and the steady drum of their hooves against the earth. It was calming. Centering.

And Charlie could use a little centering.

He wanted Daisy to stay with him, but that would require either her to change her life's trajectory or him to change his. And that was asking a lot from the both of them. Charlie wasn't an idiot, he knew it was too soon for him to talk about forever with her, and yet his heart could only dream of forever.

Ugh.

He rode faster, really letting his mount fly along, and the horse had no problem picking up speed. Although Archer wasn't anyone's specific horse, Charlie had always liked the girl. She'd been a rescue, and her name wasn't from his family, but they kept it nonetheless. Apparently, she used to belong to a traveling performer group and her owner had been the trick archer, which was how she'd earned her moniker. But the owner had suddenly passed from cancer. The performance group had tried to keep her, at first, but it became clear that without her bonded owner, Archer wasn't interested in performing anymore.

She was loyal like that, but it was clear that sometimes she missed the rush of streaking by at top speeds.

She ran a good long while before Charlie finally slowed her to a walk. Although Archer was impressively fast, she could push herself too hard and needed her rider to be mindful of the limits for her.

Now that Charlie thought about it, he was pretty sure she wasn't the only one with that issue, Cass coming right to the front of his mind. But hey, at least she was doing a lot, *lot* better after he'd had that real talk with her and she'd gone on to hire Mick.

Huh, I never realized that I was the one that set that off.

But he had. If he hadn't called Cass on her constant boundary-pushing and lack of self-care, he didn't know if she would have stopped. He loved Cass; he did. He admired her too. But the second eldest was about as stubborn as a mule and ten times as independent, which made her less than an easy patient.

She really had come far. And her perseverance was part of what kept Charlie from quitting when he wanted to. Because sometimes, he did. He wanted to rebury his trauma until he could just pretend that it didn't exist and just hide out on the ranch until he was old and gray. But if Cass could fight past all the insane, painful obstacles in her path... well, he could too.

Easier said than done, of course.

"Nothing good is easy. Few things that are easy are good," he reminded himself. But man, he sure did miss easy.

Lost in thought, he let Archer walk for several more minutes before slacking the reins. She knew what that meant, that it was almost time to run again, and he could feel her perk up with excitement. But before they quite got there, he spotted something odd a few yards up ahead.

"Hey, Cici, that you?" he called, leaning forward and shielding his eyes from the sun.

They were in the absolute hottest part of the summer, so it was unusual to find any of his siblings outside between one to three, and yet his youngest sister was laid out under one of the shade trees they used to always play under when they were young. There had once been a tire swing there, attached to the sturdy arbor, but the rope had long since rotted and come down.

"Hey, Charlie," she responded, not even sitting up. She managed a slight wave from the blanket she was lying across before going right back to her previous position. But something about the entire thing seemed off, so Charlie urged Archer to gently trot toward her.

Cici had grown so much since she'd gone off to college. Charlie wasn't going to pretend like she wasn't babied by all of them. How could they not? She'd been so young when their mom died, had held her hand as she passed, and she was possibly the one who's suffered the most from it. She ran the whole gamut from night terrors where she would scream, hurt herself, and sleepwalk. She had violent panic attacks. At one point, when things had gotten really bad, she'd had a sudden onset of a disorder and couldn't walk.

They'd put her in therapy, of course. Gotten her a whole team of experts. And the entire family had gone to therapy along with her, both individually and as a family. It was a concerted effort to get Cici healthy, and that had kind of stuck with them all.

Not that Cecilia ever took advantage or anything like that. In fact, Charlie knew that sometimes she felt guilty about all the energy she took up. But every one of her siblings would do it all again and more if it meant she was okay. It wasn't her fault that her body reacted how it did to trauma, and it was clear that she was trying to—

Oh.

Oh.

Okay, suddenly Charlie was connecting some parallels between him and his sister that he never had before.

That was unsettling.

"What're you doing?" he asked once he was close enough, getting off of Archer and giving her permission to go graze. She was a good horse, so she wasn't liable to run off somewhere she wasn't supposed to be.

"Oh, you know," Cici said, making a vague gesture. "Enjoying some sun, feeling the breeze, nursing a heartache. The usual."

"A heartache?" Charlie blinked. Had he missed out on something? But then his mind turned to the worst and his gut just about twisted in two. "What's going on? Do I need to go get a shovel? Tell me where he is."

That got her sitting up. "Whoa, whoa, Charlie. Nothing like that. No shovel needed. I promise."

That settled him down, but only a little. Sure, he hadn't been able to hang out with his little sister since she'd gone off to college, the first one of them to get her four-year degree. "Do you want to talk about it?"

"There's not much to talk about. I like someone. I've liked them for a long while, but if there ever was a window, I missed it. I didn't tell him how important he was to me, so I can't blame him for it. It's all me." She flopped back down, sighing. "I wish I hadn't let my fear get to me, but I did. So now I've got to face the consequences of being a total weenie."

Charlie felt his expression soften. Oh, little Cici. So full of energy, joy and excitement for pretty much everything, and it seemed like she was stricken with the same Miller self-doubt that was going around. "A total weenie, huh?"

"Yup. A total, absolute, colossal weenie. An extra yellow chicken. A particularly cowardly dog—"

"I get it." Charlie sat down next to her and fished some carrot sticks out of his pocket. It wasn't chocolate, but his gut instinct told him that if one of his sisters was upset, he should feed them something.

Huh... maybe Clara had a bigger influence on him than he realized.

"Are you treating me like a particularly upset horse?" Cici asked, eyeing the carrot.

"Fine, if you don't want it—"

"I never said that!" She took the carrot and bit into it, the stick giving off a very satisfying crunch. Her eyes widened at that and she let out a contented sigh. "Oh man, I missed home-grown produce. The stuff they have at the mess halls just isn't the same."

"I imagine it wouldn't be."

She nodded absently, continuing to chew her carrot. They sank into silence, sitting under the shade tree and just looking out at their lands.

There were so many stories around them. Written into the ground, lingering in the air, etched into every fence and dug into every hole. But all of them were a comfort to him, even the melancholy ones. They were the ties that made the ranch home.

"So, what are you going to do?"

"Huh?" Cici asked, blinking like she'd entirely forgotten he was there. Granted, given it was Cici, that was entirely possible.

"About your heartbreak."

Her brow furrowed in that cute way of hers that just screamed 'little sister' to Charlie, and she was quiet for at least a minute or two. "I suppose I'm just going to let myself feel it, then I'll move on. And the next time I'm lucky enough to meet someone I feel this way for, I'll fight for them."

"Fight for them?" He adored his littlest sis, but she was about as peace-loving as they came. While Charity would throw a hook if anyone dared insult any of them, Cici was more of a diplomat.

"Whatever it takes. I know next time I can't expect it to just be handed to me because I want it really, *really* bad. Besides, he seems happy, and if I *really* loved him, then that should be enough for me."

Charlie was staring and he knew it, but something in her words clicked with him. Cici was a lover, not a fighter. But she was willing to fight for love the next time it comes around.

That was powerful.

And if his baby sister could do it, then why couldn't he?

It was scary, the thought of losing Daisy because their paths were diverging, but he owed her honesty. He needed to let her go or nail things down. He needed to be brave for her.

Be brave…

"Are you okay, Charlie? You're really pale."

"I'm just thinking. You learned some pretty cool things at college, Cici."

"Glad you think so. Sometimes I wonder if I just took the spot of someone who deserved it more."

"Cici, if there's anyone who deserves to chase her passions, it's you."

"Awww, since when did you learn just what to say?"

"I guess I've been going through some schooling myself. A bit more informal, but I've learned a lot."

"Oooh, maybe I should go there next. Informal schooling."

"I think you're on your own path."

"You're probably right."

They sat a while longer before Cici finally let out a long breath and stood. "Alright, I've soaked up enough rays. I'm going to go eat a whole container of ice cream, put myself to bed and then greet tomorrow a new woman."

Charlie had to chuckle at the imagery of his sister in her over-sized pajamas surrounded by empty ice cream containers. "It's that easy, huh?"

"Easy? You try downing half your body weight in dairy before you make any comments about difficulty."

"Wait, aren't you lactose intolerant?" Normally they kept a good stock of dairy-free products, but Cici hadn't really been home long enough for their order to come in.

"Exactly."

And then he was laughing. When had his little sister gotten so funny?

He didn't know, but she just clapped his back to get up, then gathered her blanket before flouncing off, her head tilted toward the sky.

"What about you, Archer? You ready to go in?"

She let out a wuffle that was very much to the negative.

"Alright. I could use a bit more of a run. You game?" She leveled a look at him that was packed so full of personality that he was laughing yet again. "Alright then. Sounds like a plan."

He got up into the saddle and gave her the signal to go off. And go off she did. Cici's words floated around his head as they ran, wind in his hair and rushing past his ears. He felt that familiar sensation of freedom rising up in him, pulling him up out of the fear and into the realm of what was possible if he was just brave enough.

The future stretched out in front of him while his past trailed behind him. He kept urging Archer on, leaving all that darkness, all that shame where they had been and not where they were running to. For so long, he'd thought that was how he *had* to feel, and ever since Daisy had offered a different possibility, he'd been too afraid to seize it with both hands. Like he was afraid it was too good to be true.

But finally, he was ready. He was ready to dream again and dedicate himself toward a future he hadn't known was possible.

He rode. He rode and rode until the sun was setting and Archer finally slowed on her own, nickering that she was done. He took her to the barn, gave her an extra good brushing, and indeed fed her every single carrot and pepper slice that had been in his pocket.

Well, except for the one that he'd given his sister.

Once he was sure that she was well taken care of, he pressed a kiss to her forehead and made his way back home.

He didn't know when it had gotten dark. Last he knew, the sun was only just beginning to set. But it was pretty nostalgic to see the ranch lit up in the increasing dark, summer stars shining brightly. The ranch was full of a sort of life it hadn't had in a long time, and he couldn't help but feel it was because of all the extra love they'd managed to pack into it.

Charity, Alejandro and Savannah.

Cass and Mick.

Even Clara and Nathan.

Maybe, just maybe, there was room for Charlie and Daisy too.

But there was something he had to do first.

"Hey there, son," Papa said from where he was sitting in a rocking chair, a steaming mug of tea in his hands. Charlie didn't miss that it was the bear-shaped one that he was pretty sure was a gift from the librarian. An inside joke between the two about him being a teddy bear. And somehow, that simple little mug gave him the last bit of motivation Charlie needed. "You missed dinner."

"I had a lot on my mind."

"You alright?"

"I'm on my way there," Charlie answered honestly before drawing in a deep breath. "But, uh, Papa, I..."

"Yes, son?"

"There's been something I've been needing to tell you for a long time. Would you take a walk with me?"

"Of course. Whatever you need."

23

———————

Daisy

"**P**ut your hands together for none other than lil' rootin', tootin', spicey and dicey, Miss Scarlet!"

Daisy took a deep breath then rode out. She was wearing the outfit Clara had made for her for the very first time, and she really wanted to impress.

The crowd went wild, the season long enough that they knew what Scarlet could do for the most part. But even the regulars were going to be in for a surprise, because Daisy was riding with Turnbuckle, which was Hermin's sweet as pie but very talented horse.

Normally, riders had their own horses that they lived with, trained with, poured everything into, but there was no way Daisy could have ever afforded to do that. So luckily, there were some other options for workers like her. First were riders who had trick horses that they loved, but the riders themselves were injured and couldn't do any sort of horseback tricks. Turnbuckle wasn't one of those cases, but Juliet was.

Then there were the riders who retired but still liked to train trick horses for movies or other productions. They would instill the basics and teach the horses tasks, but horse actors needed to be able to do the task with anyone, so exposing them to multiple riders was a great benefit to them.

And then there were the sponsors, which was Turnbuckle's situation. Sometimes people just wanted to see talented people ride talented horses and would donate performances out of their mounts. Well, Daisy supposed 'donate' was the wrong word since they most definitely got paid, but either way, it made sure she always had a reliable, trained horse to ride. She did her best to stick with three or four as much as she could for an entire season.

"Let's give 'em a show, my boy."

And that was exactly what they did. He raced forward, turning on a dime around the first barrel and charging toward the next while hardly losing any speed. From there he turned around the second and cut across the field in a direct line. It was a classic maneuver, but one of the most difficult because it involved intense turns instead of trying to mitigate both the speed and the torque on the horse's body.

Another sharp turn and down to the bottom, then the last turn and to the original barrel. The crowd cheered again and thus began the trick portion.

Daisy pulled out pretty much everything she felt safe doing. She stood in the saddle, rolled off the right side and pretended to run along beside the horse before pulling herself upright. Then a handstand in the saddle before eventually doing an upside-down front split.

And, just like she hoped, the crowd lost their minds. It wasn't a trick she used often, if only because jeans weren't really flexible enough for her to pull it off. But the slacks that Clara made? Perfect. They didn't pinch at her inner thigh or tug at her knees, allowing her to slip into the move gracefully and like it was the easiest thing to do in the world.

It wasn't.

But the audience didn't need to know that.

Then she took to the ground and grabbed a rope that one of the clowns tossed to her. She always liked the comedy part of her act, and it gave both her and the horse a chance to rest. Sure, there were still tricks to be done, but they were easy ones and mostly revolved around either chasing or lassoing the clowns then forcing them to jump into barrels.

It all went flawlessly, and when it ended, Daisy's heart was swelling so much it felt like it might be an actual medical problem. She took her bows, Turnbuckle took his bows, and then they triumphantly went 'backstage' together.

"Wow, you really killed it out there," Rick said, running in from the ring and dropping the false barrel that he was wearing. She could hear the laughter coming in from the door and couldn't help grinning herself. Rick had great physical comedy chops.

"Thanks! You did too, as usual."

"Aw, coming from you, I appreciate that." He flushed and gave her a tip of the head before hurrying off to his next task. He really was a good guy; she hoped he found the girl he was dreaming of soon.

Like usual, she felt refueled by the energy of the crowd and her own success. When she was flying so high, it was easy to forget why she ever needed alcohol so much, and for a few moments, she was just a normal human being.

She would have to cling to such moments the next time she was feeling low. Because as nice as it was to think that she'd just be good forever, addiction didn't work like that. No matter how hard she tried there would be highs and lows. The important thing was that she was honest with herself and kept up with her coping mechanisms.

Granted, that was a lot easier to do with Charlie and the Millers by her side.

...too bad they would be going away soon.

That thought definitely made Daisy's floating mood sink, and she found herself chewing her lip as she brushed down Turnbuckle.

Moving an hour and a half further southwest wasn't a relationship killer, but that was only for a couple months. Then she would be going another three hours west until the entire rodeo season ended.

And then...

Well, and then she only really had her trailer to live in, but she usually stuck around California because it was someplace that she didn't have to worry about freezing to death overnight in her trailer.

She didn't *have* to stay in California, however. She could come back and just crash somewhere on the Miller land with her trailer. But she knew that the Millers were *very* traditional Christians, and she didn't want to insult them by being an unmarried woman requesting to live on their land while dating their son. The last thing she ever wanted to do was insult them. Not after everything they'd done for her.

Ugh, she really needed to find a way to talk to Charlie, but every time she tried, she sort of locked up. Everything was so magical that she didn't want to possibly ruin it. She'd ruined so many things in her life; she didn't want to do it again.

Conflicted, she headed back out to her trailer so that she could change before she ate lunch. She was so protective of her new outfit from Clara that she wouldn't eat in it unless she could cover herself completely in a blanket.

But she was just barely halfway there when she spotted none other than Charlie himself. She raised her hand to wave, expecting him to come greet her. It was his day off. He'd probably gone to therapy or spent more time on the ranch, so she figured that he was just rolling in for an impromptu lunch.

She personally treasured those meals together. And not just for the delicious food he brought her. Not that the food wasn't appreciated. Every day she felt like she was stronger and could think more clearly.

But it was his company, and the fact that he drove for an hour and a half to the rodeo and back to the ranch, that always made her feel so incredibly valued.

A lot of what he did made her feel more valued than she ever believed she could. More than her mother told her she ever deserved.

He didn't come toward her though. He didn't even seem to *see* her. Instead, he just beelined straight towards the head coordinator's office.

That was weird.

Curious, Daisy went to her truck's cab and just sat in the back, watching so she could catch sight of Charlie when he left. She expected it was probably going to be a few minutes, but then ten minutes passed. Then fifteen. Then an entire hour.

That was far too long to spend in the makeshift building.

That was far too long to spend in the space, even with air conditioning, and she couldn't help but wonder what could possibly be going on.

In the end, it took another twenty minutes before Charlie finally came striding out, looking quite determined. Like she'd expected before, he marched straight towards her, beaming once he saw where she was.

"Hey there, gorgeous lady," he said with a grin. "What'cha doing out here?"

Daisy didn't want to tell him that she'd been watching him, so she busied herself with jumping out of the cab and landing in front of him with plenty of fringed flourish.

"Just getting some air. Had a really good show today."

"Aren't they all good when it comes to you? I've never seen you fumble a number."

"Flatterer. But this one was *really* good."

"I'm glad to hear it." He leaned forward and planted a light kiss on her cheek, and Daisy felt that familiar warm flush go through her. She loved that he trusted her with that, even if she wanted more, and it made her feel so appreciated every single time. "I know you've got to get out of that, toss some hay, and then do the goodbyes with the crowd later, but are you free tonight?"

"Why, yes I am. You got an idea?"

"You could say something like that. Let's grab dinner, okay?"

"You bet," Daisy said with a resolute nod. "Pick me up at my front door?"

"Sounds like a plan." Another kiss on the cheek. Two in one day? He was going to spoil her. "See you soon."

"See you," Daisy murmured, her heart dancing in her chest. She hadn't been so excited for a meal in a long while.

"Charlie, this is a steakhouse."

"Yeah, I imagine that's why the sign out front says 'Verona's Steakhouse.'"

He was wearing that smirk on his face that he had whenever he was being snarky, and he was *so* lucky that he was cute.

And funny.

And charming.

And wait, what were they talking about? Right, the restaurant.

"Charlie, I've heard about this place. It's like, over fifty dollars a plate. And that's for the cheap stuff."

"You don't worry about that. You mentioned that you needed some more iron in your diet, so what better way to do it?"

"Uh, broccoli and iron for one. Not steaks that cost a day's pay."

But then Charlie slung an arm around her shoulder and that vulnerableness leaked into his voice again. "Hey, don't worry about the money, okay? I really like taking care of you, and it would make me very happy if you'd come into this restaurant with me and enjoy whatever your heart desires."

How could she ever say no to that?

"Alright then, but you owe me."

But he was dead serious when he responded. "Yeah, I do."

Did he know how he made her heart thunder, or was he just wreaking havoc on her cardiovascular system on accident?

She didn't know, and she certainly didn't get an answer before they were greeted and then sat down at their table. It certainly was a swanky place, nothing like the few western or cowboy-themed dives that she occasionally treated herself to on those rare times when she had twenty or so dollars to spare. There was mood lighting, and some older paraphernalia with little plaques that gave info about it. The servers weren't dressed in kitschy cowboy outfits, but rather black slacks and various colored button-ups with a single state flag patch on them. Apparently, they were supposed to be either the server's favorite state or where they were born, or at least that was what Daisy was told when she asked their server why they had Hawaii on their chest.

She thought she'd feel terribly out of place, but she wasn't. Sure, she wasn't about to kick off her shoes and sit back, but she didn't feel on edge either. So, it was easy to slip into conversation, to talk more about her day and how amazing Clara's outfit was. Charlie listened, like he always did, and Daisy felt like she was the center of the world.

But at the same moment, it made her feel so terribly sad. Soon, they would have to part ways. The magic that she was holding in her hands was going to be gone, and she was too much of a coward to risk everything to ask for more.

Because whenever she had something good, she wanted more and more and more until she made herself sick. She didn't want to abuse Charlie's goodness or everything the Millers had done for her, but she didn't want to let them go.

"Daisy?"

"Hm?"

"Did you catch what I said?"

Daisy blinked at him, realizing that she'd sunken so deep into her melancholy thoughts that she hadn't been listening at all. How self-defeating. Her time with Charlie was running out, so she needed to cherish every single second that she could.

"I'm sorry, I drifted off there. Could you repeat it?"

He chuckled uncertainly. "You're making me nervous."

"I am? Why?"

"No, it's not important. It's that I, uh…" He paused to take a drink of water, and now Daisy certainly found her attention thoroughly on him. Was he breaking up with her? Telling her that this was their goodbye dinner? It was too soon! She wasn't ready.

But that wasn't what came out of his mouth at all.

"I was just asking if you'd feel like it was smothering if you ended up having to see me every day."

What?

Daisy sputtered for a moment, the conversation going completely the way she hadn't expected. "What? No! That sounds like an amazing time to me."

"Really?"

Her eyes were shuttling all over his face, trying to figure out what he was getting at. She could feel that something very important was happening, but she didn't want to hope. She didn't want to hurt herself like that. Hope was dangerous, if only because she was a twin to disappointment.

"Yeah, I mean that with all of my heart," she said.

"Well, that works out well then, because I've joined the rodeo circuit for the rest of the year."

"What?" Daisy tried to jump up, only for her knees to slam into the bottom of the table and she almost knocked over both of their drinks. Whoops.

"You okay there?" Charlie asked, a grin back on her features.

"That depends on if you're pranking me or not right now."

"I would never joke about something like this. These past months have been better than I could ever ask for, and I'm not ready to give that up yet. I want to get to know you more. I want to grow closer to you. And I don't feel like we can do that states apart.

"But if I'm being truthful, I recognize that I'm on a journey right now, a journey to heal a wound in me that I've let fester for years, and I'm scared I can't make it without you."

Goodness, her poor heart. Daisy found herself reaching across the table, taking his hands in hers. "Oh Charlie, you're strong enough that you absolutely could, I know it. But I'm honored, truly honored, that you would want me by your side for something so important.

"And if *I'm* being honest, I've never felt so comfortable in my recovery. I haven't had a craving for a beer in ages and I really think that I could break my last record. And that's because I feel safe with you. I feel supported. Believe me when I say I'm *not* ready to give that up."

Her voice cracked at that, but she refused to let herself cry because she didn't want to miss a single expression that passed across his face. Because losing out on a single detail was absolutely unacceptable.

"I'm really glad to hear you say that," Charlie said, sounding like he was about to cry too. They were a mess, weren't they? But she didn't care. Everything that she didn't dare hope for was happening. Was she dreaming? It felt like she was, but when she squeezed his hands, he squeezed right back, rooting her in reality. "Because right now I'm going to say something crazy."

"Something crazy?" Daisy's heart was beating in her throat, trying to imagine what else he could give her. She already was going to have him until the end of the entire season, all the way to California. It was more than she could ever ask for. "How crazy are we talking?"

"I'm talking about crazy enough to suggest that, if the rest of the season goes really well, we could look into possibly getting you a permanent trailer on the ranch."

What?

Daisy could only stare, her brain going offline for several solid seconds.

He wanted her to move in with them? He wanted her to be part of the Miller family?

Her mind was overwhelmed with all of the possibilities. Waking up early and taking care of the chickens with Clara. Bottle-feeding babies when the goat mothers had triplets or didn't take to milking. Helping Cici or Papa Miller weed in the garden and eating all of Clara's cooking that was available.

And her brain just kept on zooming. She envisioned more fittings and outfits in Clara's workshop. Learning more of Cass's organizational system so she could help Charity. Cutting wood. Clearing fields. Bonfires. Feeding pigs. Turning over compost.

She could see it all and she wanted it. She wanted it so *badly.*

"Are you serious right now?"

"Yes. Incredibly. And if you need time, I understand. I just want you to know where my mind is, and although we've only been dating for a couple months, I can't help but think of forever."

She couldn't stop it, the tears welling up and streaming down her cheeks. The people around them were going to think that he was either breaking up with her or proposing, and they couldn't be further from the truth.

Daisy *felt* like she was being proposed to, however. Funny, how she'd never been much of a crier until Charlie rolled into her life with all of his grand gestures and affection. It was like he was so good that he was a constant shock to her system.

"Are you really willing to give up your whole cushy life for months? You're going to be so far away from your family and everything you love."

"No, not everything I love. Because I'll be with you, and that's where my heart is."

On anyone else, it would have been cheesy. But to Daisy, it was everything that she needed to hear.

"I really, really hope you're in the frame of mind to kiss me right now, because if we don't, I might just explode right here and now," she said.

He grinned at her, looking just about as happy as she felt. "Yeah, I would say I'm definitely in the right frame of mind."

That was all she needed to hear. Daisy leaned over the table, her lips pressing against his. They weren't making out, not by any means; that wouldn't be polite no matter how happy they were. But they kissed and kissed, gentle pecks on the mouth at first until Daisy moved onto his cheeks, his forehead and even the tip of his nose. She wanted to smother him with affection, to shield him from everything dark until he could see just how amazing he was. Even if it took forever.

Yeah, forever sounded *real* nice.

They didn't pull away from each other until someone cleared their throat, and Daisy sat back when she realized their waitress was standing there with her dessert.

"Sorry," Daisy murmured; except she wasn't sorry at all. And apparently Charlie wasn't either, because when they made eye contact, they both burst out laughing.

It took a while to calm down, their dessert sitting between the two of them while they talked about all their plans. But she was perfectly fine with that. Because she was hand in hand with Charlie and that was exactly where she wanted to be.

And, for the first time ever, she now knew exactly where she was going to stay.

EPILOGUE: DAISY

"Come on, it's just a few more miles. You can make it, baby."

Daisy swore that her truck groaned in response, the entire frame rattling like it was personally offended by her very existence. But it kept going, slowly slugging down the dirt road with the last of its gumption.

Normally that would have been horrifying to her, a countdown to tragedy. But Daisy didn't care because, very, *very* soon it wouldn't matter that her truck was basically a rusted-out bucket that was hanging together by bubblegum and a whole lot of prayers.

Because she was on her way to Charlie's ranch, the rodeo season over and the rest of her life waiting ahead of her.

Not for the first time, she was struck by the disbelief that everything was real. If Past Daisy could see just how good Current Daisy had it, she wouldn't believe it.

But it was true, certifiably true, and Daisy was on her way to finally see it for herself.

Charlie had taken off three weeks earlier to do all of the last-minute preparations. Daisy wasn't sure how many last-minute preparations could go into a single trailer, but apparently it was a lot because he had only replied to her texts twice since the morning, one wishing her safety and the other saying to call when she pulled into the ranch.

But still, she was pretty excited. Charlie's RV was huge, and she was very much looking forward to the upgrade. Especially since she was going to have her own bathroom. How wild! She was pretty sure that her incredulity that any of it was real was the only reason that she wasn't vibrating right out of her own body.

Finally, the sign to the Ranch appeared in the distance, like a golden billboard leading her home.

She finally had a home.

Grinning, she grabbed her phone and dialed up Charlie. She knew she shouldn't technically talk on the phone while she was driving, but she was alone on a dirt road that only led to the Miller Ranch and that was it, so she made an exception.

"Hey sugar!" she said, grinning brightly even though he wasn't even beside her yet. "I'm pulling up to the sign right now."

"That was fast. Alright, stop there. We're coming to get you."

"We?" Daisy asked, eyebrows going up.

"Yeah, we."

And then he hung up.

"Millers and their sense of drama." She sighed to herself, still smiling so hard it hurt. In the months since she'd gotten to know the family, she'd learned just how much they loved a good surprise and a good gift. She was literally spoiled within an inch of her life, and she would be forever grateful for it.

Ever since she'd left her mother's house, she hadn't had a vehicle, a phone and a balance in her bank account all at the same time. But with all of the family's help, she was doing better than ever. She'd even started to put some away into a savings account, and she was saving it to get Charlie a really great present for his birthday.

But still, she knew better than to steal the joy of whatever the Millers were planning, so she pulled to the side of the drive and threw her truck into park. She was pretty sure the vehicle swore at her in a dying rumble before it finally went quiet.

It didn't take long before she saw the welcoming party approaching down the road that led to the cabin-mansion. And it was most *definitely* a party, containing several cars and she was sure all five of the Miller siblings.

Huh, now that she thought about it, she'd never seen all of them in one place with both Papa Miller and that nice librarian lady who would occasionally pop by.

...and they had balloons, didn't they?

Oh yeah, they had balloons.

"Welcome home, Daisy Dixon!" Charlie said from the *literal megaphone* that he was holding, grin evident even from all the way where he was. And where he was, was standing up in the Jeep with his upper body sticking out of the open roof.

"Dear Lord, you sure made something special when you carved that one," Daisy said, shaking her head and getting out of the car.

The whole convoy pulled up and Charlie jumped to the ground, practically bounding over to her. There was something else in his other hand. She realized that it was one of those giant hearts with specialty chocolates inside. And knowing Charlie, it certainly wasn't the artificial, cheapy chocolate that she'd had to resort to.

"Hey there, gorgeous," he said, leaning in and kissing her

cheek. And just like the very first time, she flushed with happiness and heat. Goodness, she loved him. "Glad you could make it."

"I am pretty in demand, but I manage to make time for the little people."

"Little people? I don't think any of us have been called anything like that in ages."

"You called me Little Bean less than ten minutes ago," Cici called, halfway hanging out of another truck.

"Hush you!"

Daisy tilted her head back and let herself laugh, really laugh. She hoped that the Millers could hear all the joy in her voice, as well as relief. She'd missed them all terribly. She knew that didn't really make sense, considering that she'd only spent a handful of weekends with them over the first part of the summer, but that was the case. They were her home, through and through.

When she came down, she leaned forward and kissed Charlie on the cheek right back. And, just like usual, he got that same dopey grin on his face.

She loved that dopey grin.

In the months that they'd traveled together with the rest of the rodeo, they'd become even closer. At first Daisy had been pretty worried about Charlie skipping out on his therapy. It wasn't like AA where she could pretty much find a local chapter no matter where she went. But then he explained that his therapist was willing to telecommunicate with him, and she felt so much better.

And it was clear to her that he really was continuing to work on his mental health. She was content with just being by him, just holding his hand and kissing his cheek, but she could tell that Charlie wanted more. That he wanted to be normal. That he wanted to be able to *choose* to honor his vow to God rather than not being able to have a choice in the matter at all.

So, they tested the waters. They could kiss more often, and he learned how to cut the contact off if he felt himself sliding into a panic attack. They were able to sit closer together, pressed side to side, and eventually he was able to lay down on a blanket beside her and just look up at the stars.

It was the slowest that Daisy had ever gone with a boyfriend, but Charlie was also the first partner she'd had since dedicating herself to her sobriety. Most of the boyfriends she'd had since she was fifteen years old were just a way to get away from her mother or to be a source of both food and booze.

Charlie was the first one she was in love with just for love, and now that she knew what that felt like, she knew that she would never, ever go back.

"Alright, are you ready to see your home?"

"You betcha."

"Well, get in the Jeep and we'll take you there."

He didn't have to ask her twice. Daisy raced him to his vehicle, basically vaulting in, and then they were driving off.

They headed toward the mansion but, at the last moment, turned to the right, away from the gardens. A moment later, Charlie's black RV came into view, a strange sort of curtain around it, and she clapped her hands.

"Hey, that's my thing," Clara joked as she pulled over beside them.

"Believe it or not," Daisy said, chuckling. "You don't own clapping from happiness."

"I don't? Well, something needs to be done about that. Cici, call the President."

"Yeah, because the President definitely holds the patent for happy-clapping," the youngest Miller said, slithering out of the truck window and landing in a crouch. Daisy wasn't sure she'd ever seen the girl exit a car normally, but that method was certainly new.

"Alright, are you ready?"

"I feel like I've been waiting for this my entire life."

Charlie beamed at that and she beamed right back. All in all, there was so much beaming going on she was surprised that everyone didn't go blind from the happiness. Charlie held out his hand for her—*where had the chocolates gone?*—and she took it, letting him lead her towards her home.

Except... they started walking past the black RV?

"Charlie, what are you—"

"Trust me."

That was all that he needed to say. But she couldn't help but wonder what was going on as they continued moving past the vehicle. Had he put a special exit on it or something? A sort of secondary side door? She wasn't planning on moving it around, so maybe making it more stationary made sense. It would be rather nice to have a back porch.

But then she saw it, and she instantly burst into tears.

The black RV, the one she was so used to seeing Charlie in, wasn't going to be her home at all. And she knew that, because there was another RV right behind it, a double-wide one that did indeed have a porch attached to it and a mural of beautiful flowers painted onto the side.

"I... I..." her words completely failed her, and she could only stare. And cry. And also stare some more. "Is that mine?" she whispered finally.

"It is," Charlie said, his arms wrapping around her.

She was snotty, teary and practically shaking, but he didn't care. Because Charlie loved her, through and through.

"If you want it," he added.

"If I want it!?" she cried, laughing through the tears. "How could I not!"

"I mean, you haven't seen the inside yet."

"He has a point," Cici called from where she was still standing a bit away.

"Ssshh, Little Bean, give them some space." That was Papa Miller, of course, and it was their voices that drew Daisy out of her tears and into her excitement.

"Let's go see it then!"

Stepping out of Charlie's hold, she gripped his wrist and pulled him along. She knew that the inside was going to be amazing, and yet she was still shocked when she flung open the door and pulled Charlie in with her.

It was *beautiful.* Done up in subtle whites, blues and grays, it was bright enough where it reminded her of a summer day, but it wasn't the same extreme colors that Scarlet was so known for. While Daisy did love vibrancy, that wasn't her whole identity. That was more Scarlet's thing.

Daisy spun in a circle, taking it all in. She could see a bedroom all the way at the end of the RV with a mattress that was truly *huge.* She knew that she was going to sleep like a brick on it, and if she wasn't about to burst from excitement, she would have tried it out right then and there. The room had windows on all sides, with gauzy blue curtains hanging over them and then darker opaque curtains beside them to block out the light.

She also saw a door that had to lead to the bathroom, a sitting area with a couch built into the wall and an *actual* table. There was just so much room!

And the crème de la crème, better than she could ever imagine, was the actual kitchen area. It still had all the limits of an RV, of course, but it was clean, spacious and had a full fridge. Not a mini-fridge. Not a cooler. But a giant, chrome refrigerator.

And it had an *ice dispenser* in the front.

Daisy had always wanted one of those, and she remembered thinking that was the pinnacle of wealth when she was a child. And yet here she was, in an insanely expensive RV, with her very own ice dispenser.

Insane.

"The verdict?" Charlie asked from behind her, sounding like he was nervous. Daisy had no idea how he could be, because it was better than anything she could have ever dreamed up.

"It's perfect!" she cried, jumping toward him and flinging her arms around his shoulders. Normally she would try to be more careful when embracing him, but caution was gone to the wind. She kissed his lips. She kissed his cheeks. She kissed each eyelid, his nose and then all along the chin. "You didn't have to do this. I can't believe you did."

"Come now, surely it's not so insane for a man to want to pull out all the stops for the woman he loves."

As amazing as it was, the entire RV fell away and she could only stare at Charlie. Although it was the second time that he'd uttered it, she hadn't heard him say it since that fateful night when he'd shared his trauma with her.

"You really love me?" she heard herself whisper.

"I do, Daisy. I love you more than I ever knew I have the capacity to love. And I'm sorry I waited until now to say it, but I wanted to make sure I was healthy enough to be everything you deserve."

"*Charlie...*"

She was still whispering, afraid that if she spoke too loudly that everything around her would vanish like a dream that she couldn't get back again.

"I can't promise that I can ever be 'normal.' I can't promise you the intimacy that most people take for granted. But I can promise you that I'll try. That I'm going to continue to work through everything that happened to me. Because I want to hold you. I want to kiss you all the time. And someday, I want to marry you and build a family with you.

"But it's going to be a long road. And I've learned from you that even with the best intentions, there will be struggles and failures along the way. But I promise, whenever I fall, I'll get up again. Because I want to. I want to be good enough for you."

"Oh Charlie, you're already so much better than I could ever hope for. I love you. I love you with all my heart, and I want to build a future with you."

He grinned at her, his arms wrapping around her waist. "In that case, wanna seal the deal with a kiss?"

"More than anything else in the world."

So, they kissed, and even though they soon had to part, Daisy was the happiest she had ever been in her entire life.

And she still had the rest of her life to go.

EPILOGUE: CHARLIE

Three Months Later

Charlie was used to life on the ranch usually moving at a pretty slow pace. There were certain months that were fast no matter what, usually the summer and fall harvests and sometimes Christmas, but the rest of the time followed the same general patterns.

But since Daisy had started to live full-time on the ranch, it was like everything was going at super speed. There was always a new experience around the corner, a new beautiful memory to be made and to treasure forever. Before Charlie knew it, three months had passed and spring was rolling in again.

It was insane.

He'd kept up with his therapy the entire time, of course, and he was past the half-year mark. For six months, he'd been ardently working on himself and learning to live with what happened to him. To move on and do all the things he wanted to do.

But just like both Daisy and his therapist told him, there were definitely pitfalls along the way. Sometimes he was so frustrated that he had to put so much work into enjoying something so many men around him never had a problem with, and sometimes he felt like he wasn't progressing fast enough. But every time he faltered, Daisy and his family were always there to help him get back on track.

And he was immensely grateful for that.

He was much better, especially with touch, but he still did occasionally slide into panics. But the good part was that he learned coping mechanisms for how to get out of panic mode so he wouldn't melt down into a panting mess. He never expected it, but Cici was the one who helped him the most with that.

Wild.

It had taken a long while, but eventually he'd told all of his siblings what happened. He wasn't explicit, and he was vague on the details, but they knew that he'd been sexually assaulted at a party and had never told anyone because he'd thought they'd be ashamed of him. It had been a heavy conversation every time, but in the end, he felt closer than ever to his sisters. They were sad that he'd had to carry that burden for so long, but they were happy that he was getting the help he needed.

"Tell me if I'm understanding you, Charlie, but I believe what you're saying is that you haven't had an incident in over two months, even with regular physical intimacy with your partner?"

Charlie felt his cheeks heat up. "Geez, when you say it like that, you make it sound like we're tumbling into bed on the regular."

"Have you?"

"What? No!" Charlie appreciated his therapist's confidence in his healing journey, but that was a goal that was still a long way off. And although he was working very hard to be able to truly *want* that kind of relationship, he was still determined to keep his vow. He wanted to give that gift to his wife on his wedding night. Not because he thought he was filthy or dirty without it, but because it was something *he* valued and wanted his life partner to know that he'd given her something that could only be given once. "We're able to kiss for a while usually."

"Can you define a while?"

"Aren't we getting a bit personal here, doc?"

His therapist just nodded amiably. The guy was a kind fellow, but he was so even-keeled during appointments that sometimes Charlie felt the guy was completely unflappable.

"You never have to tell me something that makes you uncomfortable, Charlie. I'm just here to help you however you need to be helped. I would just like some clarification on where you're at, because sometimes you use terms I'm not familiar with, or slang that has a different meaning to me."

"Ohhh, right, you're from the islands, right?"

"There are many islands, but I am from Haiti, yes."

"Right, right. That's why you speak French."

Finally, Charlie got a surprised reaction out of his therapist in the form of a single raised eyebrow.

"I don't recall ever speaking French with you."

"You haven't, but you've got a bunch of French psychology books all on your shelf, but they're scattered randomly meaning you don't view them that much different than English. Pretty common in polyglots with their second and third languages." Charlie squinted slightly. "Although, I suppose if you speak

Haitian Pattois, English and French would actually be your third and fourth languages?"

To Charlie's surprise, his therapist laughed. A real, hearty laugh. "You continue to delight me with your wit, Charlie. You truly are a highlight of my day."

"Oh geez, doc. I'm already paying you. You don't have to butter me up."

"Don't worry, I will be nothing but truthful with you. And that is why I will remind you of the subject that you are trying to avoid with humor. According to you, you haven't had an incident in weeks. Your longest streak yet?"

Time had been going so fast that Charlie hadn't realized it had actually been that long. "Yeah, I guess that's true."

"And you're not avoiding your partner?"

He thought back to a star picnic they'd had the night before, laying side by side with a bonfire right beside them, a heavy comforter over them to keep them warm from the lingering bite of the start of spring.

"No, definitely not avoiding."

"Then I'd like to ask you something."

"Yeah, you do have a habit of doing that."

"Now, if you don't know the answer, that is perfectly fine, but I want you to think on it and tell me what you conclude during our next session."

"Alright, sounds fair enough."

"Can you say why it is that you're able to be physically intimate with Miss Dixon, either with holding hands, hugging or kissing, but you are still struggling with even platonic contact with other people?"

Oh.

He hadn't expected that question.

And he didn't know why. It was a fair question.

"I mean, that's easy. It's because I love her."

But that apparently wasn't the right answer. "I'm glad to hear that, Charlie. But love is a complex thing, and more a combination of many, many emotions and beliefs. I want you to dissect it more than that. Try to find a root of what really sets Daisy apart from everyone else."

"Why?"

"Because if you can find what makes her special, I believe you can apply it to other people in your life. Perhaps a friend from the rodeo. I believe you mentioned a nice gentleman named Rick?"

"No offense, doc, but I'm not exactly looking to kiss on Rick."

"No, but I imagine you'd like it if he could clap you on the back without going into a panic. I imagine you'd like to hug your friend without your skin crawling. Or have him be able to sling an arm over your shoulder without sending you into a flashback."

"Okay... that all does sound like it'd be pretty nice."

"Exactly. So again, if you don't know, that's perfectly fine. I just want you to try to dig deep and examine what makes her special."

"What if she's special just because it's *her*?"

"While I believe that Miss Dixon is indeed an incredible woman, the reality is the boundaries of your trauma response lay only with you. Daisy sets you off less than anybody else because of you, not her."

That made Charlie sit back, and he tried his hardest to think about it. Really think about it. It was so easy to list off about a billion and one things that were amazing about her. Her smile. Her skill. Her intelligence. The way she looked at him. The way she fit in so well with his family, it was like she was always meant to be there. It went on and on and on.

But why... why didn't he react nearly as badly with her?

He thought about the last time they kissed. The last time they hugged. He thought about every time his blood raced around her, and it slowly began to come to him.

"When I go into these panics, or when I go back to... *that* time, it's because something in my body thinks it's unsafe, and it goes on full alert instantly."

"That makes a lot of sense to me, Charlie."

"But when I'm with Daisy, I feel safe."

"You feel safe?"

"Yeah, somehow, I trust her. I know that she would never purposefully hurt me. When I look at her or into her eyes, I feel refuge. She's my haven, you know?"

A slow, genuine smile spread over his doc's umber-brown features. "I believe I know exactly what you mean. It sounds like, to me, that trust is the root of your ability to get close to Miss Dixon. Next week, I'd like us to work on ways for your friends around you to establish trust in the same way."

"You really think that will work? I can be normal?"

"Normal isn't a real thing. No one is normal. But if you are asking if you will be able to be the average man, no, I do not believe so."

Oh... that was a bummer.

"You may always need some space. Strange women physically touching you might always make you incredibly uncomfortable. But I do believe that you can have strong relationships with a healthy circle of friends and not violently react or feel sick when they touch you."

"And all because of Daisy?"

"All because of *you*, but it does seem like your lovely partner is the key."

The key, huh? That... that felt right.

His appointment continued, but after another ten minutes or so, it was time to head back home. But when Charlie ended up on the street, an idea came to him.

But he needed help.

On his walk to the parking garage, Charlie whipped out his phone and dialed up his eldest sister.

"What do you want this time?"

"Love you too, Charity. Are you busy today?"

"For once, no. Savannah and Alejandro are still on their science retreat thing and I'm surprisingly bored."

"That's what you get for having a daughter who's basically a genius."

"She's not my daughter yet. The lawyer said it would be better to file her adoption paperwork after we're married."

"That's just a technicality. You know she's your little girl," Charlie said with a smile on his face.

He heard Charity give a wistful, loving sigh on the other end of the line. "Yeah... she is. My genius little mad hatter."

He loved that his sister's relationship was going amazingly. After the terror with her ex, Alejandro was a welcome relief.

"Anyways, why did you call?"

"I need your help with something."

"Oh? What's that?"

"I want to pick out a ring."

There was silence on the line long enough for Charlie to reach the Jeep he shared with Clara and hopped in. "Are you talking about... an engagement ring?"

"Well, I didn't spontaneously develop a new interest in custom jewelry."

Charlie had to pull his phone away from his ear as his sister screamed. And just when he thought there was a break, he heard Cass in the background faintly ask what was going on. Charity answered, and then she was screaming too.

"Hey, guys, I'm kind of trying to keep this a secret, so could you maybe not announce it like fire sirens?"

"Huh? Oh, right. Right. But yeah, I'll help you."

Charlie grinned, putting his key in the ignition before checking the time. "So, how fast can you get to the city?"

There was more noise on the other end before Charity answered. "Cass says she wants to come too."

"You're the one driving her here."

"Alright. We'll be there in an hour and a half. Text me where you want us to meet you."

"Will do."

"Oh, and little brother?"

"Yeah?"

"I'm really proud of you." She hung up, and Charlie felt happiness bubble through him.

He was proud of himself too.

"Happy Birthday to you, Happy Birthday to you! Happy Birthday dear Daaaaaaiiiiiisy, Happy Birthday to you!"

Charlie was a ball of nerves, feeling like he was going to sweat right out of his clothes or fall over. But even with all that going on, when Cici started to sing "How old are you now," he did manage to quickly look at her.

"You finish that sentence, and you will be banned from all the birthday cake," he warned, winking.

"You don't have the authority," Cici accused. College really had made her smart.

"You're right," Clara said, passing by them with a platter of cupcakes for other guests who didn't want the lemon cake that Daisy had requested. "But I do, and you won't see any sweets for a month."

"This is tyranny."

"No, this is my birthday," Daisy said, grinning cheekily from where she'd blown out all the candles. "Now someone come serve this to me before I perish."

Several guests laughed around them, but not Charlie or his siblings. All of them were in on his plan and he imagined that they were just as nervous as he was. Luckily, they weren't the only attendants of the birthday party, so they didn't have to carry the ruse solely on their backs.

There were his cousins, Bart and Missy, as well as Silas and Elizabeth. They hadn't brought their little ones, however, as Aunt Annie had demanded to babysit some of her grandkids before she mutinied and started putting too much salt in her famous biscuits. Charlie wanted to take Daisy up there sometime, but between AA, settling in, and the rodeo ramping up again, there was a lot on their plates.

Melinda and Billy made it too, and Raph of course. But the big surprise was Jeremiah and Rick.

Oh, and Rick's pretty new girl that he'd rolled in with.

Good for him.

"Cut the cake," Daisy said, clapping her hands on each word, and soon she had a good and proper chant going through everyone who wasn't Charlie or his siblings.

"Alright, alright. Hold your horses. As the love of your life, I will make sure you're served, my lady."

"*Oooh,* my lady. I feel so fancy."

He rolled his eyes and she stuck out her tongue, but it was just what he needed to break the tension inside of himself. He loved Daisy with everything he had, and he wanted her to have that ring.

He just had to hope that Clara hadn't messed up.

Going over to the cake, he picked it up from in front of Daisy and moved it to the cutting area that Clara had already set up. According to his sister, the ring was located right in the center of the heart at the bottom of the cake, and that was the slice he had to give Daisy.

He really, *really* hoped she didn't swallow it. But Clara assured him the cake forks she'd ordered were so tiny that there was no way she'd be able to take a big enough bite to obscure the jewelry.

It took a lot of willpower for his hand to not tremble as he cut into the confection, and he was glad that his back was turned to her. And after about an eternity making sure that he did every-thing perfectly, he nodded to Clara. She caught it and strode forward with all that effortless grace she always had.

"Alright, who wants lemon cake and who wants cheesecake cupcakes!?"

Hands went up and with both Cici and Charity's help, everyone was served, forks at the ready.

Everyone but Daisy.

"And this is for you," Charlie said, setting the plate in front of his love.

She grinned at him, her expression as soft as ever. "Don't you want a piece?"

"I'll have some later."

"So you're just going to watch me eat?" she asked.

"Yup."

"Weirdo."

"The weirdo that you're in love with."

"You got that right." She winked at him then finally dug her fork into her cake, everyone else following suit.

It was torture watching her go through the thick slice with that tiny, microscopic, little fork. It seriously tested Charlie's patience, and it was only his intense desire to see her face when she found it that stopped him from just blurting out everything.

And then it happened. Daisy dug her fork in, and it clinked against something hard.

"Uh... there's something in here," she muttered, a look of total confusion on her face.

"There is?"

"Yeah. Hold on, let me just—" She dug further into the cake then became dead silent as a small, heart-shaped case tumbled out onto her plate.

Barely bigger than an indulgent chocolate, yet the sound it made managed to quiet the entire party and all eyes went to Daisy.

"Is this..."

When she raised her head to look at him, her eyes were already watering. Charlie felt his throat constrict, but he managed to grin back at her. "Why don't you open it and find out?"

She didn't say anything, her mouth dropped open. When her hand did move, he noticed the tremble as she picked it up and cleaned it off with her napkin.

For once in her life, Daisy Dixon seemed to be absolutely

speechless as she opened the case, revealing a golden band there with three glistening diamonds mounted at the center. And that was his cue.

While she was still staring at the ring, Charlie knelt beside her, one knee down and his hands over his heart.

"Daisy Dixon, you are the most incredible, amazing partner that I could ever ask for. We've both grown so much together, and when I'm with you, I feel like the future is limitless. I don't think I can ever go back to a life that you're not in, so would you do the honor of staying with me forever?"

"Charlie..."

He hadn't heard her voice break like that since she'd first seen her trailer. And just like before, she moved so fast that one moment she was in her seat, and the next she was on the ground as well, her arms around his shoulders.

"Yes, yes, *yes!* I'll marry you, Charlie Miller!"

Then she was kissing him.

And he kissed her back. He kissed her with all the promise he could, of tomorrow, the day after that and the day after that too. And she clung to him with her considerable strength, letting him know that he was safe, that he would be there for him for the rest of his life.

Cheers erupted all around them, and eventually they broke apart to stand and wave. But their hands stayed intertwined, holding onto each other. The future was uncertain, full of responsibility and surprises, but Charlie knew without a doubt that they would always have each other.

"Let's give it up to the future Mr. and Mrs. Charles Miller!" Rick cried, lifting up his glass of sparkling apple cider. If anyone noticed the complete lack of booze at the party, they had the good sense not to say anything.

"Cheers!"

Charlie didn't have a drink, so instead he just kissed his girl—his *fiancé*. And she kissed him right back, promising him the world.

They'd been on a rocky road, sure, but now that they'd found each other, Charlie knew they'd never be apart again. They had a whole future ahead of them, filled with so many things, but not fear.

And he couldn't wait.

~

Hello reader! I hope you enjoyed Charlie and Daisy's love story. The next Brides of Miller Ranch, N.M. story has a bit of a lighter theme and what seems to be a reader favorite... best friend's brother romance! Cici had a crush on her best friend's older brother all throughout her school years. Now he's back in town and newly single. He's handsome mechanic who just got his heart broken and guess who's there to help him pick up the pieces!

You can find Cici and Baz's sweet romance on all major retailers. But if you haven't given my bookstore a go yet, I'd love for you to give it a try and support my small business. Scan the QR code below (might be on the next page, depending on the book format) to be taken to Cowgirl Fallin' for Her Best Friend's Brother at Natalie Dean Books. If scanning QR codes isn't your thing, you can find my store here: nataliedeanbooks.com Just look under the Miller stories tab for Brides of Miller Ranch, N.M., and you should be able to find this book.

ABOUT THE AUTHOR

Born and raised in a small coastal town in the south, I was raised to treasure family and love the Lord. I'm a dedicated home-schooling mom who loves to travel and spend time with my growing-up-too-fast son.

When I'm not busy writing or running my business, you can find me cleaning house, cooking dinner, feeding our three rescue cats, trying to make learning fun and coaxing my son to pick up his toys. On less busy days, you may also find me paddling down a spring run in Florida, hiking a mountain trail in Georgia (on the rare vacation to the mountains), or enjoying a book.

If you love Natalie Dean books, you can be notified of new releases by signing up to my newsletter at nataliedeanau thor.com, where you will also receive two free short stories for signing up. Just click on the "Free Books" tab at the top and you'll be on your way!

Also, as previously mentioned, I've opened my own online bookstore and I'd love your support! As of June 2024, I'm selling my ebooks at Natalie Dean Books. By late summer or fall 2024, I should have audiobooks, regular paperbacks, large print paper- backs, dyslexic print paperbacks and signed paperbacks all avail- able. At the request of my loyal readers, I'll also be adding merchandise, such as glasses, cups, magnets and more. So come check out my small mom-owned author business at nataliedean books.com.

You can also scan the QR code below to be taken to the home page of Natalie Dean Books.

facebook.com/nataliedeanromance